CURIOSITY KILLED THE WITCH

AN ENGLISH ENCHANTMENT WITCH MYSTERY
BOOK 1

MARA WEBB

———————

*a*rson is no joke, I get that, but I considered it. A small fire that would set off the alarms, but not one that was big enough to actually burn the place to the ground.

Somewhere in the distance a train rumbled away from the station and I considered sprinting through the door to try and chase it down, climbing aboard and starting fresh somewhere else. That wasn't going to happen though, I wouldn't be allowed to go anywhere until my shift was over.

"Just let me get this right, because I think I misheard you," I smiled. "You want a layer of tuna mayonnaise *beneath* the chicken, and then you want it toasted?" The guy nodded. I had to wonder about the mental state of a man that combined those things, but the customer is always right I suppose.

I would argue that the customer is rarely right actually, but we are advised to avoid arguments with the people that keep us in business. I couldn't help but look up at the clock, hoping that somehow there had been a sudden leap forward to the end of my shift. No such luck.

"Don't forget to smile, Elizabeth!" My mother was giving me stage directions from the comfort of a chair in the back of the restaurant, and I was tempted to shout back "Don't forget that you're on the clock, too!" but held my tongue. I went by Liz, and she knew it. I just wanted to be free of this place for the weekend. In a stroke-of-genius move, I had booked two days off a few weeks ago and now the time was almost here.

It isn't until you've worked in the food service industry that you can truly appreciate the need for a washing machine. Even on my days off it seemed that my clothes maintained the aroma of freshly baked bread and melted cheese. I know there are worse things I could smell of, but it's hardly ideal.

I handed over the tuna-chicken monstrosity, took payment and bid a not-so-fond farewell to the man as he left the building.

"Any chance of an early finish?" I smiled, hoping that the empty building would be indicative of the lack of need to stay open for the final twenty minutes of the workday.

"Does the gingerbread shop close early?" she replied.

"No," I huffed.

"Then I think you have your answer," she said. She licked her forefinger and thumb, pawed at the thin pages of her cheap magazine and turned to the next column of gossip. I wasn't sure what she got out of those publications. They were the type of magazine that would pay you up to five hundred pounds for a story and you needed absolutely no proof that it was true. They would pay and print without a second thought.

I could see from here that the cover story was one about a young woman that claimed to have been impregnated by a ghost. I secretly hoped she would read that page out loud when she got to it, but she was now mid-rant about the gingerbread shop. This was possibly her third one of the day.

That bloody gingerbread shop was the bane of my life. When you live in a town like Black Bridge you are likely to hear endless tales of the gingerbread shop.

Black Bridge is nestled in the English Lake District, a place famed for its beautiful views, fresh air and quaint towns that cater to the tourists that descend upon the area each summer. My family ran a small restaurant and I'd made it clear on multiple occasions that I had

2

no interest in working there. It had been my first job as a teenager, I was an adult now. Here I was yet again up to my neck in sliced baguettes.

If you have ever travelled to the Lake District, then you have probably heard about the gingerbread shop that my mom insists on dragging into every conversation. The place has been open since 1854, or so they say, and has an international reputation for producing some of the most delicious gingerbread, and related items, anywhere in the world.

I have lost count of how many school trips involved us all being ordered onto a small bus to drive over to Grasmere, only to stand in a queue for forty minutes while the teachers try to get their hands on gingerbread flavored rum-butter.

My family aren't in any way associated with gingerbread, we don't sell it in the restaurant and don't even particularly like the taste, but somehow they have all decided that the gingerbread shop is our direct competition. *Give me strength.*

"Are you heading out anywhere exciting tonight?" mom asked. I was tempted to laugh but resisted. Exciting? In Black Bridge the most exciting thing to do is leave. I'd managed it once, made it all the way to London in fact, but now I was back.

"Nothing special planned," I said. "Are you and dad still going to that town meeting?"

"That's tomorrow," she replied. "Your father is still working on a placard to hold up when the council arrive."

Who in their right mind would voluntarily attend a council meeting in their free time? Oh right, my parents, that's who. It wasn't a huge surprise that dad was still working on his sign. He had strong views, but would never back it up with strong language. It's the English way more often than not. Push all those angry feelings deep down inside and never mention it, because letting people know what you are really thinking might cause discomfort.

I couldn't even remember what the council meeting was about. A new road maybe, or *another* conversation about flood protections. The rivers flood when it rains heavily, this isn't breaking news, yet every time it happens the town council gets in a flap about how 'none of us could have seen this coming'.

We live in England. It rains more often than it doesn't.

As my mother continued to flick through her magazine, I began to quietly pack away the deli meats. Look, no one would be walking through that door before we closed, I would be willing to put money on it. I silently placed the lids back over the plastic tubs of salad items and was just about to discretely gather the sauce bottles from the tables when the door opened.

I felt my heart sink. I just wanted to leave, why would someone be walking through the door at this time? Surely they could see the sign with our opening hours, everyone knows not to bother anyone in the final thirty minutes of the work day, right?

I let out a sigh a little louder than I planned. "Sorry, is it a bad time?" a man asked.

I turned around to look at the customer that had entered, expecting to maintain my irritation for the duration of our encounter. My rage quickly dissipated as I looked at the closest thing to Hugh Grant I'd ever seen in real life.

I was clutching a handful of ketchup bottles, holding them close to the branded polo-shirts that my parents had bought for the place. It was totally black, but had a small sandwich embroidered where you would typically find a breast pocket.

Seconds ticked by as I stood speechlessly staring at him. He wasn't from around here; he had an accent that suggested he'd been to an expensive private school and he had a jawline that could cut glass. I wasn't entirely sure why I'd initially compared him to Hugh Grant, he was just the pinnacle of English romantics according to Hollywood.

I was personally more of a Dr. Who fan myself, but I would watch the occasional rom com when the mood struck. Bridget Jones' Diary is a perfect movie and no one can convince me otherwise.

"Are you still open? The sign here says..." he said. I had tilted my head sideways like a dog trying to understand human conversation.

"Yeah!" I snapped. "You've got time." I shouldn't have interrupted him, that was rude and *not* something that Hugh Grant should have to tolerate.

"Perfect," he smiled. *Urgh.* There is a charm that comes from a man that speaks well, it's hard to define why it is so attractive, it just is. I doubted it was just his accent that was doing it for me, his eyes were a vivid blue and he had the sort of floppy dark hair that looked good no matter how it was styled. He was giving off a 'Four Weddings and a Funeral' look, if I were to continue with my Hugh Grant comparisons.

"What would you like?" I asked.

"What do you think I would like?" he replied. He had a twinkle in his eye that made my cheeks blush. The gentle flirting had caught me off guard and I tensed my arms, compressing the five ketchup bottles I was holding and causing them to fire in all directions. Ketchup shot across the tiled floor, two of the tables and in a huge streak over my shoulder.

I could feel it soaking through my shirt, it was cold against my neck and it was dripping from the end of my ponytail. *Let this be a nightmare.*

"Oh gosh, do you have a cloth somewhere?" he asked.

"She can get cleaned up and I can serve you," my mom said from behind the counter. Obviously when the drop-dead gorgeous man walks through the door she is magically able to get off her chair and make a sandwich. This was probably going to be the first customer she had served all day.

"Are you sure?" he said, looking again at me to see how I was planning to deal with the sauce that was all over me.

"It's best I tackle this in private," I muttered, shame glowing out of every pore. I shuffled back around to the counter and through the door to the staff area. For some reason there was a small, rectangular mirror over the sink where we washed our hands. I almost couldn't bring myself to look at my reflection, but I did.

I could hear muffled conversation through the door as he ordered a sandwich to go and my mother asking him questions about his business here in Black Bridge.

"Nice one, you bloody idiot," I hissed at myself. "No wonder you're alone."

I couldn't bear the thought of seeing him again, so set about cleaning up the staff area, organizing the items that would be needed by whoever was working tomorrow. Thankfully, that didn't include me. I heard my phone make a sound from my bag and rushed over to see who was trying to contact me.

"Pizza and games tonight?" the message read. It was from Kari, the extrovert in my friendship group that was largely responsible for all of our gatherings. She was the interesting one, a tanned blonde with dual citizen ship. A British *and* American passport, she may as well be an astronaut.

She had an English mother but an American dad. I think she had been born over there, I couldn't remember exactly how it had happened. Due to the constant travel between the US and England, she had an accent that danced between the two countries. A huge chunk of her formative years had been spent in Maryland, so she sometimes needed us to translate ourselves so that she knew what we were talking about.

"Sounds good," I replied. If I had dual citizenship then you couldn't *pay* me to live in a place like this. Why she had settled for a small, wet town in the middle of the Lake District is beyond me, but I was grateful that she had. She was the firecracker in the group, without her we probably would never do anything interesting.

Once I was confident that the handsome stranger had left the building, I stepped back into the front of the shop and started to finish cleaning up. Mom helped, but not a lot. I just needed to get home in time to shower before I went to Kari's house, because if I showed up smelling like ketchup then she wouldn't stop talking about it for the next week.

I waved goodbye to my mother as I sprinted out of the door and looked back over my shoulder once just to make sure she had locked the door behind me. My dad was probably going to meet her there so they could walk to the pub for dinner, that was a routine of theirs. On days when she worked, he would take her out for a meal. Considering they had been married for almost thirty years, it was impressive that they still went on dates like that.

It was a short walk back to my small house, everything is a short walk from everywhere in Black Bridge. I could probably walk from one end of town to the other in less than twenty minutes if I moved quickly enough. I let myself in, locked the door behind me and charged up the stairs to the bathroom.

There was just no way to remove the polo shirt without spreading more ketchup all over myself. I pulled it up over my head and felt it smear across my cheek and forehead. I lead such a glamorous life. I balled up the shirt so that I could drop it into my laundry basket without getting sauce all over the wicker.

As I stepped into the shower, the water began to turn pink as it ran off my body and swirled down the drain. I glanced at the half-dozen shampoo bottles lined up on the shelf and contemplated which one had the strongest scent, hoping it would be potent enough to cover the condiment smell.

Within half an hour I was knocking on Kari's door. We all had a key to Kari's house, she was an over-sharer so thought nothing of letting everyone in our friendship circle have unrestricted access to her home. It seemed that I was the last to arrive. You would knock, wait approximately five seconds, then let yourself in anyway.

"Lizzie, I'm about to order!" Kari yelled from her cross-legged position on the living-room carpet. She had a laptop opened in front of her and was perusing the menu of the one and only pizza joint in Black Bridge. There *were* other options if you wanted pizza, but that meant paying a huge delivery charge for some out-of-town restaurant to send an employee over on a scooter.

"Why do you look at that thing every time?" I asked. "Surely you know it backwards and forwards by now," I laughed.

"She is convinced that they will add a new topping any day now, she doesn't want to miss out," Ed replied. Our circle of friends was made up of six people, sometimes a new partner would drift into the mix, but not for long. We were all romantically tragic it would seem.

"Well? Have they got something new and exciting for us to try? Or

7

are we going to waste thirty minutes staring at a screen before ordering a triple-cheese?" I sassed.

"Well I'm sorry for trying to keep things interesting!" Kari called, a slight American tang in her accent. Over the years we had learned that Kari would get a stronger American accent when she was annoyed.

"Is it *you* that smells like ketchup?" Ed asked. He was looking right at me.

"I showered!" I protested. The others laughed loudly enough that Kari had to step into the kitchen to place our pizza order over the phone, and I heard her ordering the same triple-cheese that we always got. "Honestly, you don't know what I'm dealing with in that place. I've clearly done something wrong in a past life to be back working for my mother."

"It can't be that bad," Natasha smiled. Ah, Natasha. She was famous for finding a silver lining where others couldn't. "After all the years apart, it must be nice to spend time together."

She was referencing my brief escape from Black Bridge when I followed a job opportunity all the way to London. I was somehow the most accomplished, and the least successful person in the room. You see, they had all followed the path to University and I had pursued an internship.

There had been an unpaid position with a newspaper in the capital and I had taken it. I wanted to get into journalism and had been assured that this was a great way to get into the field. Of course the people that had assured me of this were those that wanted my free labor.

I couldn't afford to live anywhere near the office, the cost of living in London was extortionate. It had meant waking up before sunrise almost every day, even in the summer when it got light at four in the morning, and riding a train. I'd gotten a part-time job in a health food store and it was my only income.

I'd hung on to my internship for a lot longer than I should have, patiently waiting for the day that I proved myself useful enough to be brought on to the pay roll. Every now and then they would toss me a poultry cheque for a few hundred pounds, but I was relying heavily on credit cards. It was only after a boozy office party that one of the executives let slip that they were in financial ruin, so would never be able to pay me. *Great.* I was aware that print media was taking a hit, but I'd clearly been naïve.

The whole thing was awful. I'd made a tearful call to my parents and told them that I'd made a huge mistake. They were more than willing to welcome me back into the family home and help me get back on my feet. Thankfully I didn't stay in my childhood bedroom for long as my grandmother had offered to let me stay in her place while her and my grandfather enjoyed a bevy of retirement cruises.

"I guess," I replied, realizing I hadn't said anything back. It *was* nice to spend time with my friends again, even if I was back to square one.

"Okay, he said it should be here in twenty minutes," Kari announced as she swaggered back into the room. "We can *either* play Settlers of Catan, Ticket to Ride, or…"

I didn't like the glint in her eye as she paused. "Or what?" I asked.

"Truth or dare!" she grinned.

"Oh come on, why do you love this game so much? You're the only one who enjoys themselves and we are all almost thirty," I complained. I was a vocal objector to this game every time she suggested it. The thing I didn't mention earlier when I brought up leaving Black Bridge for my internship in London, was that I hadn't just left town.

I'd been dating someone, we'd been together for a few years, but I was so convinced that the internship was my path to the career I wanted that I'd broken it off. I hadn't *wanted* to, but he didn't want to leave town. I was in a position where I had to choose between my own future, or him. I frequently consider that I made the wrong decision, but that wasn't something I ever said out loud.

The glint in Kari's eye made me think she was planning to get more stories out of me about the breakup, I'd never spoken about it much. Everyone else in the room seemed happy enough to play.

It was going to be one of *those* nights.

"Yes, I *did* kiss Ross. But in my defense I thought he was someone else," Kari cackled. She had, for some reason, taken up most of the turns in the game of truth or dare. None of us were dumb enough to choose 'dare' anymore, not after the winter streaking incident.

Kari spun the bottle on the coffee table again and I watched as the glass slowed. *Please don't land on me.* The open end of the bottle was pointing squarely at my chest and I saw the glow of excitement in Kari's eyes as she tried to think up a question.

"Are we *allowed* to ask questions about James?" she said. The sound of his name made my blood run cold for a second. It was like opening up an old wound that was trying to heal.

"What sort of questions?" I asked.

"Have you spoken to each other since you moved back?" Kari said. The jovial energy in the room had been completely sucked out, and now five pairs of eyes were staring right at me with bated breath.

"No," I answered sincerely. It was the truth, the painful, unavoidable truth. I hadn't been back in Black Bridge all that long, but I'd heard whispers around town about him. I couldn't bring myself to even risk a chance encounter, so I purposefully avoided places I thought he might be.

In a small town like this one, that eliminated almost everywhere. If I wasn't at work, I was at Kari's house or my own. I'm not sure a therapist would recommend my coping strategy but so far it was working for me.

"Do you *want* to speak to him?" Kari asked.

"I think you were supposed to spin the bottle again. You don't get two questions," I smiled. *Gotcha.* I knew Kari wouldn't be able to keep this up all night. At some point she would get bored of hounding me and we would all move on to our board games.

As she tried to spin the bottle again, clearly trying to calculate the angle she would need to try and guarantee that it would point at me again, the doorbell ring. *Thank you, universe.*

"I'll get it," Ed called. He leapt up from the floor and rushed over to collect the pizza, grabbing the cash off the table on his way. There was a large sofa in the room, but we always sat around the coffee table on the floor instead. It was uncomfortable, and we spent most of the night repositioning ourselves every few minutes to make sure we didn't cut off the blood supply to our feet.

I heard my phone buzz in my bag and I reluctantly checked to see who it was, as if I didn't already know. Even though my journalism internship in London had ultimately led to nothing, I still had learned enough about the field to be employable. Or at least that was what I kept telling myself.

Black Bridge had a small newspaper called The Herald, and I was determined to force my way in by hook or by crook. This had meant preparing many, many articles for the Editor in Chief in exchange for mediocre pay. At least it was something other than preparing sandwiches, and it stopped me from lying awake at night reflecting on my own failures. That's not true, I was still awake at night thinking about it all. It just felt better to have not abandoned my dream career entirely.

"David has just messaged me," I announced. This was met with a chorus of booing from my friends as they knew it meant I would be heading back out the door. "Can I grab a slice for the road?"

Ed opened the pizza box and allowed me to take a piece. It was far too hot for human consumption, so I passed it back and forth between my hands a few times to avoid burning off my fingerprints.

"You do know that we are all judging you for working with that idiot," Owen said. His face was full of judgement, he was the most vocal about his dislike for David. I also thought the man was a total clown, but in the interest of keeping my measly job, I kept it to myself.

"Well, judge away," I said, taking a bow. "Goodbye, farewell, I'm out!" I called, walking straight out of Kari's door and back onto the poorly lit road. I would rather spend my night playing games, but with Kari hell-bent on asking me questions about James, it might be more comfortable to tolerate David's company for an hour or two.

Despite the fact that I earn money as a writer, I have yet to find the words to describe David Dawson. He has achieved a lot in his thirty-something years, while also being the dumbest person I have ever had the misfortune to encounter. He is the boss of the local paper, but I have yet to see him work for more than six minutes straight, so how he got such a position is beyond me.

He isn't unintelligent, necessarily, but has no awareness of how to utilize his brain. There is that old saying, 'intelligence tells you that a tomato is a fruit, wisdom tells you not to put one into a fruit salad.' Perhaps it is wisdom that David is lacking.

If you told him you had visited Timbuktu, he would interrupt to say he had been to Timbuk-three. The thought of someone having something he didn't was completely unacceptable, so he would straight-up lie to your face if he thought it made him look good. He also waxed his own eyebrows at his desk, I had caught him doing that on more than one occasion, but he denies it.

Everything is a competition with him, always. He's in incredible shape, that much was undeniable. His shirts struggled to cover the girth of the muscles beneath. I had to imagine that all of the steroids he was abusing had affected his mind or something. As I stepped into the office for The Herald, our town paper, he was sitting awkwardly against the wall. *Great.*

"I thought that you promised you weren't going to squat in the communal spaces anymore," I grumbled. He was performing a wall-sit. If you are unfamiliar with this term, it is basically holding a squat with your back against a wall, as if you are sitting on an invisible chair. He tried to get us all to do it as a warmup for the day a few weeks ago. We rioted.

"I've been like this for thirty minutes!" he called. *No he hadn't.*

"Great!" I grimaced. "You said you had something important for me." If I let him, he would de-rail the conversation to his many perceived athletic achievements, so I had to bring him back on task.

"Yes, there is a townhall meeting tomorrow and I want you there," he said. His thighs were shaking as they struggled to maintain his position, I didn't know where to look.

"I thought that you had someone for that already," I replied.

"Yeah, well he's just called in to say his cat needs emergency surgery so he won't be available," David said. This was what I meant about David's wisdom deficiency. That cat had needed almost three surgeries this month alone, if it truly existed then it was knocking at death's door. I had a theory it was a fictional feline that was only mentioned anytime weekend work was required.

"Oh no, should we send flowers?" I teased.

"Top idea, Liz! Could you arrange that?" David grinned. *Urgh.* "I have a few nuggets of information about the town hall all ready to go, so I'll send those over to you. It's going to be quite lively, the council has been in talks with some development company about selling the green belt behind the church."

Green Belt was a term I had always found strange. It is a term that has been around for almost a century, but some people still aren't sure what it means. Basically, there are large chunks of the British country-side that is designated to be wild, untamed greenery around urban centers. It controls growth, or 'urban sprawl' as it is affectionately known.

It typically means that there are huge areas of natural beauty to be found almost everywhere and that no one can just come along and build five hundred houses on it. However, the green belts can be sold off for astronomical amounts of cash and most small towns spend time arguing with their local councils as to why they shouldn't take the money.

My parents were advocates for the natural land around our town, so no doubt their attendance tomorrow would be part of a crowd shouting obscenities at our elected officials.

"When do you want something written by?" I asked.

"Well the paper is out Monday, Liz," David scoffed. "So the sooner the better." Another classic, non-committal answer from him. No matter when I submit my article, it will either be far too late to make it into print, or too early and that will be somehow equally offensive to him.

David likely had a date with a set of seven-hundred-pound weights at the gym over the weekend, like a silver back gorilla. He would hate to be expected to read through my work during leg-day.

"When do you want to read over it by?" I asked.

"I trust you, I don't need to check your work," he grinned. What a lazy oaf. I was familiar with this style of management, some called it a 'hands off' approach and would brand it as a way of making sure that employees stay accountable and that they don't feel micromanaged. David did this so that he had as little to do as possible.

I was honestly surprised to see him in the office so late. There were one or two staff members tucked away in their cubicles typing frantically, while David did random body weight exercises in a pair of painfully tight corduroy trousers.

"Don't you have a gym where you can do that?" I asked.

"I'm waiting for a delivery. I accidentally used the work address for my accessories order," he replied. And there it is. The real reason David is here, as always, was because he had used the wrong address when ordering himself shoes. If he *knows* he has to be in the office, then he gets things sent here.

CURIOSITY KILLED THE WITCH

Sometimes the delivery doesn't arrive during his work hours and he is forced to wait until it does, making himself a hostage to the royal mail. It would probably be fine for him to leave and let one of the people that were still here collect his parcel, but I suspected he wanted to show off immediately and couldn't wait.

I didn't need to stay in the building now. I'd gotten the email that David had sent from his phone, so I had all the information I needed ahead of the council meeting tomorrow. I would benefit from getting home to read over it, doing my own research and showering again. Ketchup lingers, apparently. I could hear an engine outside though and knew that it had to be the delivery van. I didn't want to miss this.

"Is there a Mr. David Dawson here?" the delivery man asked as he leaned through the doorway. I raised an eyebrow at him, he was in here delivering parcels to David at least three times a week. "I know, but I have to ask," he whispered back, a smirk on his lips.

"That's me!" David replied, stretching up out of the lunge he was in the middle of and collecting the large package. He signed his name on the digital screen that the delivery man handed to him and then loudly, to no one in particular announced, "this must be the Ralph Lauren bundle I ordered." Who asked?

In a private moment, David had once told me that he ordered knockoffs of designer brands from some strange website and paid a fraction of the price. He had assured me that no one, not even Anna Wintour herself, could tell the difference. I had pointed out to him that the band of his underwear was showing, and that it read 'Calwin Klyne'. He didn't seem to have learned his lesson.

"I'm going to leave, unless there was something else," I said. At this point I suspected that I could have avoided coming into the office altogether if David had simply called and told me that he wanted me to take the council meeting assignment. I could still be eating pizza with Kari and the others.

"Don't you want to see what I've got?" he asked. It was a cringe-worthy cry for attention, but I felt sorry for him enough to delay my own free time. I'm a sucker for a sob story.

"Why not?" I smiled, pulling up a chair to the nearest table and watching him tear through the plastic bag like a child on Christmas morning. It was as I had expected, multiple belt buckles, shoes with bad-copies of designer prints, and a shirt that I had to assume was the 'Ralph Lauren' knock off. This featured a man riding on the back of a large dog, instead of the iconic polo-playing horse.

But, as I already mentioned, I'm sure Anna Wintour wouldn't notice such discrepancies.

I made the appropriate amount of approving sounds, some encouraging facial expressions and even threw in a couple of 'this is such high quality' comments as I ran my fingers over the already-disintegrating leather.

As far as I knew, David was a wealthy man. He had some bizarre addiction to fast fashion for a guy that could buy genuine, designer things. But I couldn't tell him what to do with his money. I mean, I have *tried* to make a few suggestions but he rarely listens.

I said goodnight, waved to the two people that were actually working and tried to get out of the door. David decided to follow me outside.

"So what are you planning to do with your weekend?" he asked.

"You've just given me an assignment," I replied, my forehead crinkled in confusion.

"Oh, that's right! Well, I have a trip to Prague booked so I might not be in on Monday. See you next week!" he called. He was climbing into a badly parked Mercedes and burning rubber up the street before I had a chance to reply.

What did he mean when he said he *might* not be in on Monday? Surely he knew when his return flight was booked for. What an idiot.

I walked along the street towards my house, my arms folded across my chest to try and keep some of my body heat close to my skin. It was cold outside, like always, and a thick fog was creeping into town. No matter how many times I'd seen the fog in Black Bridge, I was always spooked by it.

Unlike London, everything in my hometown was a short walk from everywhere else. Being back here wasn't all bad, but in the quiet moments when I was walking around by myself I couldn't help but miss the constant hustle and bustle of a large city. A small bus rumbled along the road with the headlights on full brightness and disappeared into the encroaching fog.

Thankfully, I had reached my door and was able to unlock it quickly enough that I was inside before the fog got any closer. I let out a sigh, locked the door behind me and stared back at my empty house. It was much bigger than the flat I'd had in London, but it had belonged to my grandmother and was still decorated to her tastes. I was grateful to have a roof over my head, even if I had to live within floral covered walls and vases on lace doilies.

I walked into the kitchen to switch on the kettle, before setting up a workstation at the dining table. My laptop was flashing with a warning that it needed charging and I was sure I'd left the cable upstairs. I'd been watching old episodes of Star Trek in bed every night for the past week, this was how I chose to spend my life as a single woman.

I jogged up the staircase and stepped into my bedroom. The decoration in here was just as intense with the flower patterns, but I had bought my own sheets, so at least the bed looked as if it was from this decade. Something was off though. Had I made the bed this morning? I was quite sure that I'd just thrown back the blankets and rolled out onto the carpet, but now it looked picture-perfect.

Had my mother broken into the house and tidied my bedroom? That had to be a new low, even for me. No doubt she would have something to say about the state of the house when I next saw her. Now that I came to think of it, I had been sure that I'd left the kitchen sink full of dirty dishes too. When I'd just turned on the kettle, the kitchen had been spotless.

I was doubting myself, so I ran back downstairs to inspect my home. Sure enough the kitchen was immaculate. She *had* to have come in and cleaned the place, but she would have called to rub it in my face by now. I had been meaning to do it myself, I swear! I just hadn't gotten round to it yet. I plugged in my laptop and turned around to grab a mug to make a cup of tea, only to find a freshly made hot drink waiting for me on the counter. Was I losing my mind?

It *had* to have been me, because unless the place magically cleaned itself then there was no other logical explanation. The sooner I went to bed, the better.

3

$\mathcal{B}$eeping car horns woke me. Is there a more stressful way to start your day than to be startled by road rage when you aren't even in a car? I opened one eye and squinted in the general direction of the bedroom window, trying to decide if it was worth getting up to see what was going on outside.

It was a Saturday, for crying out loud. Everyone knows the unspoken rules of social etiquette regarding loud noises, don't they? You never phone someone before nine o'clock in the morning unless there is an emergency, you don't mow your lawn or beep your horn either. Weekends are for sleeping in a little later, being noisy like this was downright rude.

The crinkling of papers as I rolled over let me know that I had fallen asleep in the middle of working on something, again. My laptop had slipped off the bed and landed on a pile of my discarded clothes, so was unharmed. I'd printed out a few pages of information to highlight and they were scattered all over the place. The room looked as if a small bomb had gone off.

I looked at my watch and scowled as yet another horn blared outside. I climbed off the bed and pulled open the curtains to see what was causing all the commotion. It wasn't even happening directly outside my door, but further along the street. It seemed that a queue of traffic was forming behind a bin truck, my head immediately hearing Kari calling it a 'garbage truck' every time she saw it. She loved using Americanisms at every opportunity.

The empty teacup still sat on the table beside my bed and I remembered that strange feeling I'd had when I'd seen the drink on the kitchen counter. I was so sure that I hadn't made it myself, but there was no other explanation for it. I needed to stop saying 'yes' to everything all the time, I was overworked and obviously needed more sleep.

I jogged down the stairs, slipped a coat over my clothes–I had fallen asleep in my outfit last night–and pulled some shoes onto my feet. Maybe I could be the first on the scene to find something inter-esting that I could write about for the paper. I envisioned one of the waste disposal guys opening up a suspicious bag that had been left at the side of the road, only to find body parts in it.

Obviously that would be horrific. I wasn't wishing for there to be a deranged killer on the loose, but I just needed there to be a spicy story for me to get my teeth stuck into so that I could prove myself to David. Not that he'd recognize talent if it hit him in the face.

I hadn't zipped up the coat, but wrapped it around my body and folded my arms to keep it in place. The air was nipping at my face in that sharp way that it did on cold mornings, stinging the inside of my nostrils. I could see my own breath, it was an awful time to be awake on a day like this.

I found the source of the commotion. Unfortunately, or fortu-nately depending on your point of view, there wasn't a dead body in a suitcase. The truck was unable to navigate its way around the narrow streets of Black Bridge because some idiot had parked their car on the double yellow lines outside the coffee shop. That was another thing Kari struggled with. You weren't allowed to park on double yellow lines. The car was a silver Bentley GT, my father's dream car. He loved pointing them out to me in movies, or sending me pictures of them via text.

In moments like these I would turn into my mother. "Oh, I wonder what those double yellow lines mean? It must be so hard to understand that a no parking zone applies to everybody," I muttered under my breath sarcastically. I'd always found her passive aggressive mumblings annoying as a child, but now they made total sense to me.

I wasn't the only one that had left the comfort of their beds to come out and gawp at the poor parking choices of a total stranger. I didn't recognize the car's license plate, and as the driver of the bin truck continued to shout expletives out of his open window a few drivers from the cars behind him joined in.

I walked past them all and glared through the coffee shop window, only to see the handsome Hugh Grant lookalike staring back at me. I was also able to catch my own reflection in the glass and I looked like Kate Winslet *after* she'd plummeted into the water from the Titanic.

There isn't a huge pool of attractive, available men in this town. Why would I take the opportunity today, of all days, to wander outside looking like a stray dog when such a gorgeous guy is in the area? He smiled and waved, and I considered taking the coat off, putting it on backwards and pulling the hood up over my face.

"Sorry, that's me!" he shouted as he left the coffee shop, drink in hand, and got into the car. He drove off to a chorus of angry drivers swearing at him. If that had been my meet-cute moment then I'd blown it. Oh, well obviously *that* wasn't the meet-cute moment, last night had been when we actually met and I'd squirted ketchup all over myself. How am I still single? I'm such a catch.

I kept my head low as I hurried back to my own front door. The phone was already ringing as I got inside and I checked the time. It was exactly nine o'clock in the morning, it would be my mother.

"Hello?" I answered.

"Lizzie, your father and I are preparing a roast for lunch," she began. "We need to know if you're coming so we know how many potatoes to peel."

"What time will that be?" I asked.

"Lunch time, of course. Also, your dad wanted to know if you could help him make the letters on his sign look 3D and he thinks you are the best person to ask," she added.

"I have to cover the event for the paper, I don't know if it's a great idea for me to be helping the protestors if I want to be seen as impartial," I explained.

"For crying out loud, Elizabeth Sutton!" First and last name, I was in trouble now. "Your poor, elderly father wants his only child to help him in his efforts to protect the natural beauty of his hometown. Are you seriously telling me that you are going to say no?"

"First of all, you are both in your fifties so I think you can't use the 'elderly' card yet," I sighed. "Secondly... yes, I'll help him." There was no use trying to put up a fight because I would never hear the end of it.

"Good," she replied. I could hear the smile in her voice. She could add that to her list of petty victories; one million to her, zero to me. "See you at lunch."

"Bye." I hung up the phone and looked around the house to assess whether or not I had time to take care of some tidying tasks before showering. Under no circumstances could I go to my parent's house un-showered. I had planned to shower before bed last night, my second attempt to wash the ketchup out of my hair, but I'd gotten caught up with reading for the town hall meeting.

I ventured back up the stairs to gather my laptop. Each step creaked under my weight, that's what you get for moving into a house so old. I often thought that it would serve as a good early warning system if anyone ever broke into the building when I was asleep. I'd be able to hear them coming and hide before they made it to my bedroom door.

I read over the notes I'd prepared last night and was happy with my work. I probably wouldn't even be called on to ask a question, but so long as I had something to write about then David would be happy.

I jumped in the shower and took my time getting clean. My weekend showers were always longer, it meant that I had time to shave my legs, exfoliate my skin and just enjoy the heat of the water. I don't really know why I had bothered shaving my legs at any point in the last few months, it wasn't like anyone ever saw them as it was freezing out and I was always wearing jeans.

At least when I crawled into bed alone tonight, my legs would feel silky smooth. *Lucky me.* I let my hair air-dry while I gathered up some laundry and threw it into the washing machine. Even when the house was tidy, it still looked cluttered.

My grandmother's collection of ornaments and small picture frames covered every available horizontal surface. She'd kept pictures of all of her grandchildren from their graduations, school plays and wedding days. There was a photograph of me as a girl holding a small stuffed cat toy and that was it. My one picture was taken over two decades ago.

I hadn't graduated, I wasn't married and, if the pictures were anything to go by, had done nothing worthy of familial pride since the day I grabbed onto that stuffed animal. I sneered at the photo as I twirled around the room with a duster, I should really replace it with something more effective, I was just moving the dust from place to place.

Even though I'd had nothing important to do all morning, I'd lost track of the hours. I'd been cleaning with the radio on and hadn't noticed that I was approaching lunch time. When I finally realized, I already knew that I was going to be late.

"Shoot!" I shouted, looking at my watch. I grabbed a pair of running shoes, pulled them onto my feet, threw my phone and keys into my bag and bolted out of the front door. My parent's house wasn't far away, which gave me even less of an excuse to be late. The more I ran, the sweatier I got. I really should have waited until *after* lunch to shower.

"Oh, Elizabeth, how nice of you to join us," my mother said as I burst through her door. Her sarcasm wasn't welcomed, it rarely was. "I think your food will be cold by now."

"I'm not even two minutes late!" I wheezed, looking at my watch again to punctuate my point.

"Lunch was served on time," she smiled. "Take a seat and... what are you wearing? She scanned my outfit and I gulped nervously. I was

23

wearing a 'Buffy the Vampire Slayer' t-shirt and sweatpants, this was my cleaning outfit and I had been in such a rush to get out of the door that I hadn't thought to change.

"I was cleaning!" I said defensively.

"Lizzie," my dad sighed. "Just take a seat before your mother's head explodes." Thankfully the empty chair was to the left of my dad and I would get less grief from him. I saw my mother tracking me as I walked around the table and sat down.

It seemed most of the family had made it. I had both my parents, my paternal grandfather, two great-aunts, my younger cousins and Deanna. Deanna was a sight for sore eyes among the crowd, she was the only cousin that was my age and we had an almost sisterly bond.

The younger cousins were all in their early twenties. These were the faces that I saw every day in the picture frames at my grandmother's house. A bunch of boring over-achievers if you ask me.

"Did you have a date last night, dear?" my grandfather asked. I shot him a look as if he had just brandished a knife. Why on earth would he ask me that in front of my mom? I saw the glint in his eye and I knew he was prodding at me for his own amusement. Why not play along?

"Yes, I had three actually," I replied. I heard the gravy boat slam down on the table as my mother reacted to my answer.

"Three? *Three?* Why can't you just pick one thing and stick with it?" she huffed.

"I suspect this isn't about my love life," I said. She took any and all opportunities to throw in a jab about my career.

"I just want you to be happy, to be settled. I find it all very stressful."

"I'm so sorry that *my* woes are causing you so much hassle," I mumbled.

"Why don't you tell us about the council meeting Aunt Sally?" Deanna asked. My hero. She was pulling my mother onto a different topic, it was like diving on a grenade for your brother in arms.

"I'm glad you asked," my dad interjected. "There is another buyer looking to invest in the Lake District. We've heard about American hedge funds moving in to buy up residential areas as some sort of tax haven, they never rent them out and it continues to drive up the house prices for the rest of us."

Should I interrupt to explain what I knew about the potential buyers? Probably not.

"They want to destroy the green belt," my mother announced. "Please pass the potatoes."

Deanna handed over the dish. "So you're protesting tonight?" she asked.

"Yes," Dad smiled. "We grew up here in a quiet town and we want the next generation to have the same natural beauty around them that we had. This is for you kids." My dad was the best. I got the full 'only child, daddy's little girl' treatment from him and I relished it. My mother was a little sterner, well a *lot* sterner.

"I'm covering the event for the paper," I said.

"You have a job!" mum squealed.

"Well, I wouldn't call it…" I began.

"We will be eating dessert on the good plates, Arthur," she called out to my dad. The good plates? There was no way I was going to point out that I was still working more as a freelancer if we were getting the good plates. The good plates had delicate flowers painted all over them, they were brought out for celebrations. They were rarely brought out for anything I'd done.

The mood felt elevated for the duration of the meal. One of the cousins started talking about the PhD programs that were fighting over him and I kept my eye rolling to a minimum. Another cousin, Marla, was showing off ultrasound pictures and talking about the hypnobirthing course she'd been doing.

I glanced down at my t-shirt, looking at Buffy and her friends. Buffy had saved the world a hundred times, she hadn't gotten a University degree *or* had a baby. I wondered if my grandma would have framed her picture. Maybe I needed to get into the vampire-slaying business.

"Liz? Are you listening?" Deanna asked. "Did you want ice-cream on your cake?"

"Wh-? No thanks," I said. I had zoned out and apparently we had moved onto the next part of lunch. Why my parents insisted on serving a three-course meal in the middle of a Saturday every week was beyond me. It would make me feel sluggish for the rest of the day.

"Are you okay?" Dad asked. "You seem a little spaced out."

"I'm fine," I reassured him. Was that a lie? Deanna handed me one of the good plates with a thick slice of chocolate fudge cake in the middle of it. I ate it at an astonishing speed, much to my mother's disgust, then announced that I needed to leave.

"Make sure you dress in something more work-appropriate for tonight," my mom added as I walked out the door. "You never know when you'll bump into the love of your life!"

"If the love of my life doesn't like Buffy the Vampire Slayer, then he's just some guy, mom," I smiled. "Hardly marriage material if he doesn't appreciate Sarah Michelle Gellar."

I could see her loading a retort, but I was already out the door. The sky was grey and threatening rain, I walked in the direction of my house, pulling my coat tightly around me. Despite feeling so full that I could burst, I knew that I needed to re-stock my kitchen for dinner later. I turned a corner and walked into the small grocery store, waving to the man behind the counter as I entered.

"Afternoon!" he bellowed.

"Hey Ernie," I smiled back. "Busy morning?"

"We've had six people in here since I opened!" he gasped. For him, that was a *very* busy morning.

"Wow, is there any food left for me?" I teased.

"Hopefully! I've hardly had a spare second to get out and re-stock the shelves!" he grinned. I spotted the crossword puzzle in his hand and laughed.

"I'll be back in a second," I said, grabbing a basket and heading towards the back of the shop. I picked up a loaf of brown bread, inspected the amount of seeds on the top, then put it back. Who was I kidding? I wanted thick, white bread that had the least amount of nutritional value. Maybe I could toast three or four slices later and slather a half-inch of Nutella on them... That reminded me that I was out of Nutella.

As I turned to walk down the next aisle, I was immediately confronted by the attractive man that I had embarrassed myself in front of twice already. This was strike three.

"Hello again," he smiled. "Fancy seeing you here."

"I don't normally look so horrific," I sighed. "I just want you to know that."

"I happen to like Buffy," he grinned. "I was always secretly hoping to grow up and be a watcher like Giles, is that weird?" Oh, it was weird alright, but the kind of weird that I was into. Wouldn't you fantasize about being Angel? A vampire with a six pack and a poet's eyes? Come on. The man in front of me was also reaching for the Nutella and I cursed myself for not having put on some make up or something. We were clearly soul mates.

"I haven't seen you around before, have you just moved here?" I asked.

"Not exactly," he said. He reached up to push back his hair and my jaw fell open, did he even know how sexy that was? His phone began to ring and he pulled it out of his pocket, glanced at the screen then looked at me. "I'm going to have to take this, but I hope I can bump into you again. Fourth times the charm, isn't that what they say?"

"I'm already charmed," I mumbled. He didn't hear that, fortunately. I grabbed the other bits I needed and headed back to the counter to pay. I needed to hurry home and pick out a weeks' worth of good outfits so that I was always prepared to run into my Hugh Grant-impersonator. It turned out that I wouldn't have to wait all that long to see him again.

4

*M*y grandmother's vanity table left room for improvement. The flat surface where I spread out my make-up was covered in decoupage, a bizarre hobby in which you basically glue cut-outs from magazines onto furniture. It was one of the things that she'd taken up after retiring and, thankfully, had found a love of cruise ships instead before the entire house was decorated this way.

I had put down my mascara and now couldn't find it, as if it were camouflaged. Stupid decoupage. The lighting wasn't great here either, so I wasn't able to see if my foundation was blended properly with my neck, or if my blush was too harsh. I'm sure my mother would be the first one to point out any aesthetic errors when I got to the town hall though.

A light drop, then another, indicated that the weather forecast had been correct. It was raining, like it often did, and I had wasted thirty minutes trying to curl my hair. As soon as the rain landed on me the curls would be ruined. I don't know why I bother. I mean, I knew why I was bothering *tonight*. There were three main reasons.

The first reason to look presentable is that I was attending this town hall meeting in an official capacity as a reporter. I wanted to look professional, I was hoping that if I did a good enough job that David would take me on full time at the paper and I could kiss my part-time job at the restaurant goodbye.

The second reason to be so delicately applying eyeliner, was that the Hugh Grant man of my dreams could be there. He had said, out loud, that 'forth time's a charm', which I was taking to mean that maybe he would ask me out for coffee. Maybe I should ask him out? Why wait around?

The third reason was James, my ex-boyfriend. I had managed to avoid him successfully since my return to Black Bridge, but my family made sure to keep me in the loop with his career and personal life. He was an officer at the town's station, just like he'd always wanted. It's a quiet place, very little crime and a slow pace that meant policing here was easy work.

My mom had also made sure to inform me that James was currently dating Victoria Cressley, a stunning blonde that stood at five feet nine, pixie features and a lucrative career modelling for small town magazines. She also had inherited a sizeable amount from her late father, but apparently attributes her wealth to her own work. I couldn't imagine that 'model railway monthly' paid much, but it was none of my business.

I jogged down the stairs to look for the smartest raincoat I owned. I pulled it on over my arms, making sure the satchel over my shoulder was covered so that it wouldn't get wet. Hood up, shoes on, time to leave.

The streets of Black Bridge were shimmering as the rain coated the tarmac roads and glistened under the streetlights. I passed houses, an old church, a veterinary surgery and a gym promoting a 'bikini-body bootcamp'. The town was an endless mass of streets, alleys and shortcuts; each journey from A to B could be made in a million ways, but to get to the hall you always had to cross the tracks.

Somehow every time I needed to get to the other side of the train tracks the warning lights would start flashing, the barriers would descend, and I would be forced to stand still for ten minutes as the approaching train chugged by. The time between the barriers coming down and the train showing up was often several minutes, and I always thought about making a break for it, dashing across the tracks quickly.

Theoretically, there was plenty of time so that I could get across without being flattened. It was one of those intrusive thoughts that came to mind whenever I was stood in the rain waiting for the barriers to move again and let me across. I never dared try it, though. My parents had told me every cautionary tale you can imagine about how dangerous it was to risk darting across a level crossing. As always, I stood patiently in the rain and waited.

As the barriers lifted, I could hear voices behind me. Half the town seemed to have decided this meeting was worth attending and we were all making our way to the same place. The protesters voices were growing louder as I approached, the placard I'd help my dad to create was being thrust skyward as he yelled about climate change, which I wasn't sure was applicable to this issue.

"Elizabeth, you could have put on a little make up," my mom chastised.

"I did!"

Arguing with her is generally pointless, but if I don't even make an attempt to defend myself then she will spin out of control.

"You look ready to take down the corporate elite, sweetheart," my dad smiled.

"Thanks? You do remember that I am here to report on the meeting, I'm not picking sides here dad."

"You're a good girl with a good heart, I know you won't be able to resist siding with us. History has it's eyes on you," Dad grinned.

"Don't quote lines from Hamilton at me dad, it's not going to work this time." I was letting the 'girl' comment slide, I didn't want to get into a whole thing about my parents seeing me as an adult woman. I didn't have time for that tonight.

"I'm just saying, you know what to do for the best," he said, turning his attention back to the suited men that were climbing the stairs into the hall. "Get out of here scum! Take your money and shove it!"

"Dad!"

"These fat cats need to know that we won't stand for it, not here," he countered. He was still yelling, making sure he was heard over the booing sound that was following the executives through the double doors. I had assumed this would be a more civilized affair, but it seemed that the gloves were well and truly off.

"They can't take those fields, they just can't," Mom muttered.

"I'm going inside, are you coming?" I asked. The swarm of protesters were now packing up their flasks of hot tea and following the suits into the building. If I didn't hurry up then there would be no space left.

Black Bridge was a village, it was designed by someone with a village mentality and so most of the oldest buildings were built to cater to a small population. The 'urban sprawl' that my parents were so against had already happened here once before, expanding the village into a town with a few hundred more houses on the outskirts.

I had cousins that lived in the newer parts, so it wasn't like my whole family was up in arms about housing development. They just seemed to have an issue with *this* proposed expansion. My parents lived in the older part, their house was one of the first things built in Black Bridge, as was my grandmothers. That was why it creaked so much when I walked up the stairs.

All this is to say that the 'town hall' as it is now known, was originally a village hall. The census from three hundred years ago stated that Black Bridge had a population of three-hundred and eighty-one people. Now that population clocked in at close to five thousand. The village hall was definitely not equipped to handle that many citizens coming into a community meeting, so it was first come, first served.

As I didn't need to pack up camping stools or take a placard back to my car, I was able to get a head start on many of the protesters and skip my way up the steps and through the doors before them. It was already busy inside, bustling with conversation and the sound of chairs squeaking along the old wooden floor. It was now standing room only for the late arrivers.

The stained-glass windows were steamed up with condensation and the men on the small stage had removed their coats before sitting down. The number of bodies in here was causing the temperature of the room to climb, and I unzipped my coat to let some air get to my skin. I didn't want to be sweaty on top of rain soaked.

The Lake District, or at least the south side of it where Black Bridge was, has fifty-one councilors. Of that group, only one was a Black Bridge native and he was not particularly interested in re-election if his recent activities were anything to go by.

I'm sure once upon a time that Stephen Berry was popular with his constituents. He had run a successful campaign if you look at the outcomes only, he was elected after all. He *actually* won because his opponent was so utterly unlikeable that it was pretty much a one-horse race. I can barely remember a single campaign promise that Stephen had made, something about recycling maybe?

I watched as Councilor Berry took center stage, lowering himself into a chair and producing a gavel from a briefcase. There was no need for that man to own a gavel. Flanking him on either side were a few councilors from neighboring towns, two men in suits that I had never seen before and… oh no.

Sitting in a chair on the far right of the stage was my Hugh Grant husband-to-be. I knew he wasn't a councilor, which had to mean he was from the company that was trying to buy the green belt. My heart sank. It sure explained why I hadn't seen him around town before, he had just flown in to speak to the locals and try to win us over. Of course the folks that were coming here to buy up the fields had sent the most handsome man they knew.

"Heart of a demon, face of an angel," Kari laughed. She had sprung up behind me and caught me staring at the man on stage. Our fourth meeting *hadn't* been the charm.

"What are you doing here?" I asked. "I didn't think you cared about the green belt."

"I care about a whole bunch of stuff, I am multifaceted! Also, Will wanted to come and I said I'd tag along."

Will was another member of our friendship group. He was reserved, took everything seriously and had recently decided that perusing a career in local politics was the way to go. Of the six of us, he was the most passionate about the government. He often forwarded links to petitions, encouraged us to volunteer during the general elections and was considering making a run for the councilor position once Stephen Berry's time was up.

We love Will, it seems important to clarify that, but he can also be incredibly dull. Kari had decided to take him under her wing for some reason, determined to bring him out of his shell. She had told him that he would need to become more extroverted if he was going to win over the hearts and minds of the town's voters.

He was now standing beside her wearing a suit that was pressed with precision, a perfect crease ironed into the front of his trousers. It wasn't a black suit, or even a blue one. It was a deep, emerald green and had been styled with a matching waist coat. This outfit was Kari's doing, I just knew it.

"Are you going to be asking questions, Will?" I asked.

"Oh yes, I'd like to know why Councilor Berry has frauded the people of this town. I want to know if he supports the calls for criminal record checks on all candidates for elected office, because I've been digging around and he has been accused of accepting bribes in the past," he replied. "Seems that he has managed to get parking tickets deleted from the system for at least four of his friends, too. He's a crook!"

I looked at Kari and suppressed a smile. "I meant a question about *this* issue."

"Oh, well I would also like to challenge the green belt acquisition. I know he will be taking a huge stack of money from it, so I'm going to fight tooth and nail about it because—"

Thankfully, Councilor Berry started banging his stupid little gavel and cut Will off before he could progress with his monologue.

"Order in the hall," Stephen announced.

"You're not a judge!" a voice called from somewhere in the room. Laughter followed. Stephen slipped the gavel into his pocket, perhaps hoping we would forget about it, and continued.

"This meeting has been called to give you all the opportunity to speak with the fine folks at Diversity Capital about their plans for the land around Black Bridge. Once the sale goes through then they will—"

"Hey!" It was the voice of my mother, it cut through the air like a knife, there was no mistaking it. "The sale isn't going through. This meeting is for us to have the opportunity to tell you all what we think of you, you aren't talking about this like it's a done deal. I babysat you when you were a boy, Stephen Berry. I'll be dead in the ground before I let someone who's arse I've cleaned tell me what is happening in my own town!"

She's not subtle, you have to hand it to her.

"Oh, and as for 'Diversity Capital'," she continued, making large air quotes around the name of the company as if she doubted it, "I'll tell you *exactly* where you can stick your money, first you'll need to bend over and—"

The gavel was retrieved from Stephen's pocket, and he banged it on the table once again. I glanced back at my parents who were now being spoken to by a police officer that had his back to me. Was it James? I couldn't see him properly from here.

"Thank you for that, Mrs. Sutton," Stephen sighed, his face beet-root-red after having his arse discussed in a crowded room. "I would like to hand the floor over to Lionel Bassett so that he can explain the plans that Diversity Capital have for the area."

My Hugh Grant dreamboat stood up. His name was Lionel? Hmm, not quite as sexy as the name 'Hugh', which was another 'con' on the list along with *working for evil hedge fund*.

"Good evening ladies and gentlemen," he began. His accent was as charming as ever. "I just want to start by thanking you all for choosing to spend your time here tonight, it is so wonderful to see a community that are so passionate about the town they live in."

This was received well by the crowd, the front three rows of people in chairs all nodding in agreement.

"As you may have noticed from my accent, I am not from around here. I'm a city boy, unfortunately, and have only ever been immersed in the chaos of London. So to be here in your beautiful town over the past few days has been delightful. I want to start by assuring you that nothing we are proposing would challenge your way of life here, after experiencing it for myself I can see how magical Black Bridge is."

The word 'magical' seemed to get a few murmurs from the crowd. Heads turned to whisper into the ear of their neighbors. Lionel flashed a brilliant, white smile to win them over further. I suddenly remembered that I should be recording the audio so that I could refer to it later. I reached into my satchel and pulled out my phone, quickly decided that recording a video would be best.

"How much money will you get from this, Berry?!" Will yelled. The sudden outburst caught us all off guard, but Kari clapped her hands with delight.

"Yeah, word on the street is you'll do *anything* for a chunk of change!" she added.

"I think it's important to—" Stephen tried to counter.

"You'd sell your own grandmother for a paycheck!" someone else yelled.

"You all ought to be hanged!" another shouted. Okay, well this had officially gone off the rails. The angry accusations and threats came pouring out of the crowd now, surprising as many of the loudest voices were those of the elderly people in the front row. Once the first shoe was thrown at Stephen, the police stepped in to bring the meeting to an end.

A stray water bottle, cap removed, was launched Stephen's way and smacked him square in the chest, water soaking through his suit and splashing onto the papers on the table in front of him. Lionel and the other executives from Diversity Capital were also targets of random projectiles, and quickly ran off the stage as Officer James Webster loudly announced that it was time to leave the building.

His voice was so distinctive, at least to me, and I found myself transported back to the times when he would be whispering sweet nothings in my ear, his breath on my skin...

"Anyone who sticks around will be arrested, I won't say it again!" he bellowed. It wasn't sweet nothings now.

The crowd was moving like a sea of people, Kari and Will were caught in the current and I saw their heads drifting towards the door.

I backed up to a wall, trying to get a good view of the situation in the hopes of taking a few pictures for the paper.

Maybe I could sneak backstage to speak with the executives, a direct quote would be great. I hadn't even asked a question, the violence had started within a record-breaking six minutes and I'd missed my opportunity. I shuffled along the wall, avoiding the throng of people leaving and made my way to the door that lead to the 'back stage' area.

I'd been in there before, it was just a small room with a few pieces of furniture and everything had a musty smell. It wasn't the kind of place you would hang out in by choice. Stephen Berry was frantically washing his hands and his fellow councilors were packing up their things. The Diversity Capital execs were nowhere to be seen.

"If you've come in here to apologize for your mother, Liz, then I won't hear it," Stephen complained. "She needs to speak to me with some respect!"

"Yeah, I'm not here for that," I replied, my brow furrowed as I considered what he'd just said. If I apologized on my mother's behalf then she would never speak to me again. Actually, that might not be the worst thing. "I wondered if I could just ask a few questions about the development proposal, I was hoping that those guys from Diversity Capital would still be here too."

"They've left, and you can hardly blame them. They are just here to buy up some land and throw a few thousand houses up, not be terrorized by a bunch of bored pensioners with a 'not in my back yard' attitude," he said.

"A few *thousand?*"

"Yeah, and a new retail center that has a cinema and restaurants. Tourists have to drive to the other side of Lake Windemere for a cinema, but with *this…*" he paused, flapping his hands to air dry them as he scanned the room for a towel, "this is a good thing for the town, all the businesses would get a boost from passing trade, and the sale itself would be a massive cash injection. We could fix all those potholes, replace faulty traffic lights, you name it! The people around here don't know what's good for them, they'll come around."

"But everyone would hate that, you saw those people out there," I exclaimed. He paused and regarded me. "They will fight this every step of the way."

The other councilors were willing to speak to me, but Stephen was done. He sat in the corner brooding as I wrote down a few statements, trying to mask my feelings about the proposed developments as best I could. In the lead up to tonight's meeting there had been no mention of adding thousands of houses to the outskirts of Black Bridge. If people were angry before, then they would be beyond furious when this got out.

5

The rumor mill in Black Bridge operated a little faster than the newspaper. After the town hall meeting, I had ventured home with a plan to review the footage I'd captured and type up some quotes from the councilors. I had instead been forced to answer a call from my mother who was now at fever-pitch.

"Where are you?!" she yelled.

"I'm at home, why are you shouting?"

"Your father and I saw you wandering off to speak to Stephen and his friends." They aren't his friends, but whatever. "What did he say?"

I took a deep breath and thought about what exactly I *should* say. For a moment or two the only sound was the ticking clock in the living room. "I don't know if I can tell you."

"Elizabeth Sutton," she barked. "What are they putting on that land if they get hold of it?!"

"Houses, shops, a cinema…" I blurted. There was no need to mention that Stephen had said *thousands* of houses. It would double the population of the town, the traffic would be unimaginable, I didn't want to be the bearer of bad news when it was *this* bad.

"You have got to be joking! I heard someone say they were putting up another railway station so that people travelling by train could bypass Black Bridge all together!"

"Well I didn't hear—"

"They are going to put some giant, soulless sandwich franchise there, aren't they? We'll be penniless!"

"Just hold on—"

"Our lives are ruined!"

She hung up, the ticking of the clock the only sound once again. It was late now, so I knew a giant cup of coffee was a bad idea, but boy did I need one. I figured a herbal tea would be a better choice, so moved my laptop onto the coffee table and wandered into the kitchen to switch on the kettle. Before the water had even boiled, my phone was pinging with a dozen messages.

Kari's text showed up first. *'Dude, your mom said the family business has been sabotaged. Are you okay?'*

One from Will, *'Did Stephen tell you that they are building new railway? How much is he getting paid to sell us all out?'*

A couple from my dad, *'If the business goes under, we have savings. It's going to be fine,'* and *'we really need to speak to your grandmother.'*

How fast had my mother spread the word? It wasn't even accurate information, and I knew that by the time the Monday edition of the newspaper was out in print, everyone's minds would have been corrupted by gossip.

I poured the hot water over a chamomile tea bag. My mother had a weird authority in this town. People were always willing to listen to whatever it was she had to say, respecting her opinions and following her example. In most towns you have a group of council members that are officially in charge, and then the person you speak to that actually gets things done. Around here, my mother was that person.

The town hall had started well, but after she started yelling at the councilors it seemed that everyone else felt free to do the same. Although she'd not made any threats, those had come from other people. Maybe they just got carried away.

I didn't need to have the article written tonight. David was hardly going to be sitting at a computer waiting for my work so he could read it. He wasn't the type to burn the midnight oil. I had the bare bones of the story, I just needed to flesh it out in the morning before sending it off and enjoying the rest of my weekend.

I closed my laptop on the way through the living room and carried my tea up to bed, each step groaning under my weight. *Old house.* I changed out of my clothes, washed my face and started to apply some retinol serum that Kari had recommended. I had only been using it for about two weeks, so couldn't claim to have noticed any difference in my skin yet, but Kari assured me that this was the key to looking like J-Lo when I reached my fifties.

I climbed under the sheets and lay down, no longer enticed by the warm drink on my nightstand. The sound of James' voice was still ringing in my ear, and I was annoyed with myself for giving it so much thought. You never forget your first love, right? Well now we lived in the same town again and he was taking up an increasing amount of my brain.

I should have stayed here all along, been with him and lived happily ever after. But would I have been happy? I was taking a chance on myself, and sure, it didn't really pay off, but I didn't want to spend my life riddled with regret. He had moved on, so I should too. Somehow.

I closed my eyes and tried not to dwell on the myriad of things that *weren't* James-related. I thought about the train tracks, the smell of ketchup in my hair from the day before, the taste of pizza with friends. James. The shouting at the town hall, the shoe flying through the air at my Hugh Grant impersonator. James.

It wasn't long before I was asleep and a strange dream began playing in my mind like a movie that I was both watching, and starring in. It was one of those dreams where you were standing in a house that you understand to be your house, even though it doesn't look anything like you remember. I was standing in the center of the living room and my grandmother was sitting in the armchair smiling.

"How are you liking the place?" she asked.

"I… it's fine," I shrugged.

"Nicer than where you lived in London, that terrible neighbor with the noisy dog that barked all night. You must be thrilled to have gotten back to quiet Black Bridge!"

"How do you know about that neighbor? You never came to see my apartment in London, I mean it wasn't really *in* London. Hardly anyone can afford to live—"

"You think I never visited?" she smirked. What was that supposed to mean?

I looked around the room and considered for a moment that I was in a lucid dream, a fantasy in which anything was possible because I was actually safe in my bed fast asleep. I nodded knowingly. "Right... well it's been fun, but I'm going to head out and go flying in the clouds or make myself appear on the front row of the Magic Mike live show in Vegas." I headed for the door, but when I tried to pull it open it wouldn't budge.

"You didn't think I would put all this energy into being in your brain just for you to wander off, did you?" she chuckled. "My body is on a tour of the Greek Islands as we speak, but my spirit is here with you, darling."

"What are you talking about? How many Mai Tai's do you get on that ship? Is it one of those 'all-inclusive' things?" I asked, for some reason replying to her as if what she had said was true.

"Well your grandfather is in a Zumba class right now, so I had some spare time."

"A Zumba class? Isn't Greece two hours ahead of here? Grandad is doing a Zumba class after midnight?" I snarked, raising a brow at her. Hey, she wasn't really here, so I could be a sassy as I liked.

"You don't understand cruise life, the fun only stops if you do. There are activities going on around the clock, and you know that your grandfather loves to dance. He doesn't hate being fawned over by women in their early sixties either," she laughed.

"Why did I have to pick tonight to have a crazy dream? I'm exhausted," I sighed.

"Your mother shouted at the town hall meeting I take it?"

"You *know* she did. Half of Black Bridge started throwing things and—why am I telling you? You're a figment of my imagination, you know everything I know." I slumped onto the sofa and let out a long breath.

"From what I gather, there is a group of city slickers trying to destroy the final resting place of our ancestors. Those fields are important, Lizzie, you know they are."

"Ancestors? What are you talking about? You think we have relatives buried in random fields outside of the village?" I leaned back so that I could stare at the ceiling.

"I thought your mother would have clued you in by now, I've been gone too long it seems."

"Tomorrow I'm taking sleeping pills, I want to be knocked out like a zoo elephant. No weird grandparent visions, just good old-fashioned nightmares about high school or that one dream I keep having where I'm on stage with the Foo Fighters and suddenly remember I don't know how to play the guitar."

"It had to be the Greek cruise, didn't it. Why couldn't it have been that awful one that just dropped anchor off the Southampton coast for a week," she sighed.

"What?"

"I'm going to have to pack everything up, get off at the next port and fly home. Honestly, your mother has such strong task avoidance sometimes that I am surprised she can get herself dressed in the morning. She told me before I left that she had no interest in being the one to tell you but I made it clear that it was her responsibility... I don't even have the words."

She stood up defiantly and motioned for the door, turning back to see me as I watched her. She raised a hand and aimed it in my direction and I felt the fabric of the sofa brush against me as I began to rise into the air.

"Oh great, now I'm actually flying," I groaned, flailing my arms and legs as if I could swim through the air to get back to the ground.

"They say a picture's worth a thousand words, well a real-life demonstration must be worth a million."

I rose higher, now approaching the ceiling. My imagination was really working overtime on this one, I could see all the dust that had gathered on the light fighting from up here, I even spotted my old phone charger that I'd lost a few days ago. It had fallen behind the TV somehow, and I'd had to order a spare one for next day delivery because I can't function without my phone.

Why would I be dreaming about all this? I looked toward the front door and saw that my grandmother was still staring at me. She grinned, whispered 'wake up' and then disappeared. It was like an old magician's trick, smoke billowing from the spot where her feet had been only seconds earlier.

I woke with a gasp, plummeting several feet down onto the sofa and hitting my ankle on the coffee table. My neck made an unpleasant cracking sound and I rubbed at it with my left hand as I sat up to look around the room. I really was in the living room. I was wearing my pajamas but had woken up down here instead of in my own bed. I looked at my watch, it was three in the morning.

It wasn't just any old watch, it was one of those sports watches that invades your privacy in every available way. My mom and dad had actually bought it for my birthday last year and I had become strangely fond of the thing. My mom later told me that she was concerned about my heart health living in a polluted city in a high pressure environment, but even those encouraging comments weren't enough to put me off.

The little heart symbol was flashing rapidly, indicating that my pulse was racing.

What was I doing on the sofa? That feeling of falling had seemed so real, like I'd actually been dropped from a height onto the furniture. The throbbing pain in my ankle was certainly real. My watch showed me that I hadn't taken any steps yet today, the counter reset at midnight so it must mean that I wandered down here not long after I fell asleep. I didn't even know I could sleep-walk, I'd never done it before.

My phone was nowhere around me, it must still be on the night-stand by the bed. The thought of staying down here in the living room suddenly felt scary. It reminded me of being a teenager at my parents house and staying up too late, being the only one still out of bed. I would switch off the downstairs light and then sprint up the stairs fueled by terror that a monster would chase me out of the darkness.

You're never too old to be scared of monsters. The lights were off in the living room, but the streetlight outside added enough of a glow through the curtains that I was able to navigate my way to the bottom step of the staircase. I paused, flicked on the light and walked over to the TV. Sure enough my phone charger was wedged behind the cabinet.

I must have just remembered that it had been next to the TV the last time I'd seen it. Dreams are supposed to be your brain's way of interpreting random information it acquired during the day, right? That must be it. Just to be safe, I grabbed it and sprinted up the stairs, hitting the light switch on the way past so that the living room fell dark once more.

As the bedroom door swung open, I spotted the chamomile tea in the cup beside the bed. I hadn't touched a drop of it before I'd fallen asleep. No wonder I had been so restless, the crazy dream about my grandmother was probably because I was stressed out. That tea would really have been useful. I walked over to the nightstand and went to move the cup so that I could plug my phone into charge with my old cable, only... no that didn't make any sense.

The cup was still warm. I lifted the tea to my lips and the steam was still billowing from the surface, one sip was enough for me to taste the heat of it. I had made this before I'd gone to bed, but that was hours ago.

I checked the time on my watch again, as if I'd forgotten what it had shown me only minutes earlier. Sure enough it was now 3:05am. I got into bed, pulled the covers up to my shoulders and lay very still. If your legs are hanging over the bed then the monster that lurks beneath can grab you, the logic from my childhood still rang true. If I was completely covered, lying straight as a pencil, then I would be safe.

I hoped that I could fall asleep again without any more incidents. It seemed this time I was lucky.

. . .

My alarm clock buzzed at six. If little machines could comprehend violence, then this noisy device would surely know it was in trouble. I slapped at it several times before sitting up to punch at the snooze button. It was no use though; I was awake now. I must have set it by mistake, forgetting that I had time off from work for the weekend. Well, I didn't need to be in the restaurant at least.

The ache in my neck was still there, throbbing as I tried to turn to scowl at the time. I never set this alarm clock. I would set an alarm on my watch, and it would vibrate against my wrist gently to wake me up. It was less startling somehow. I don't even remember the last time I *saw* this clock, let alone set an alarm on it.

I used my phone to look up the opening time of the town pharmacy, maybe I could go there to get some of that muscular heat cream that helps with aches. Ten years ago, I would use the stuff to help me recover from sports injuries, now I needed it because I'd slept awkwardly. That's aging, I guess.

Dang, opening time was hours away. We did have a small store that opened early, a mini version of a national chain that was a direct competitor of Ernie's place. Ernie didn't open at six, though. I would usually never even consider it but given that I didn't want to spend the rest of my day trapped with neck ache, I didn't have a lot of choice.

My pajamas consisted of a button up shirt and a pair of long trousers. I managed to shimmy out of the bottoms, remove the shirt, and shuffle over the wardrobe. I knew I had a wrap dress in here somewhere, it was the perfect outfit to own when you had a neck injury. You didn't need to pull the thing over your head, just put it on like a bathrobe and tie the belt in a knot at the waist. This particular one was navy blue with a few white flowers stitched around the sleeve cuffs.

I had worn this to work in London a bunch of times, it looked very professional but took the least amount of effort to put on. After a cautious descent to the ground floor, I put on my raincoat and slipped some pumps onto my feet. If I actually bumped into Hugh Grant this morning, I'd be ready for him. Only in this case Hugh was actually a money-grabbing executive from an investment firm that was trying to take a wrecking ball to the natural beauty of Black Bridge.

I was the only one on the streets this time. Sunday was the day that everyone silently agreed to treasure, a day dedicated to slow starts and big breakfasts. The chill in the air was icier than it had been when I'd been rudely awoken by car horns the day before. It was still dark, and I was relying on memory to guide me around town.

I planned on picking up any high calorie snacks I could find after I'd grabbed the muscle heat cream. Maybe they had those pastries that are ninety-percent cooked and you just pop them in the oven for ten minutes before gorging.

This particular store was, again, on the other side of the train tracks. It was a longer walk there than it would be to Ernie's place, but he didn't open for another few hours and I couldn't wait that long. Soon I turned the corner that brought the level crossing into view. The barriers were down and the lights were flashing. There was a train on its way, but something was very wrong.

One barrier was in the correct position, but the other was wedged upward slightly as it was caught on the front of a silver Bentley GT. It was parked across the train tracks and the lights were off, but the dim light from the sky made it clear that there was a person inside. A figure slumped in the passenger seat.

A noise like nothing I'd ever heard suddenly screamed out into the air. The approaching train was trying to slam on the brakes to avoid a collision and I felt myself throw my hands against my face in complete shock. *Please don't hit the car!*

I shouted, "move!" as loudly as I could but the screeching brakes were too loud, I could barely hear my own voice. I felt a jolt of energy in my abdomen, a feeling I put down to an abundance of adrenaline racing through my body, and then the screeching grew to a crescendo as the train slowed dramatically.

By the time it reached the car it could barely have been travelling at five miles per hour. The collision was gentle, or as gentle as it could have been, and the car was slowly flipped and pushed off the tracks down the grass embankment just beyond the crossing.

A crowd of angry locals had all raced out of their beds to air their grievance to whomever was causing such a raucous at this time, only to find a freight train in a stationary position with a driver leaping from the engine car screaming, "I've killed him!"

6

*K*eep calm and carry on, it is the British way. Once the initial shock had subsided, many of the ogling specta-tors retreated into the comfort of their warm homes. I had never seen a train hit a car before, the image of the Bentley on the tracks, the screeching of the brakes still ringing in my ears... it was over-whelming.

The train driver had been offered a mug of tea by the lady that lived in the house closest to the railway, and he was gratefully sipping at it with a trembling hand. I heard her mutter something about 'fetching him a blanket' as she shuffled back towards her front door in a pair of lilac house slippers.

That train had been going at full speed. It was a freight train, one that passed through Black Bridge without stopping. It was impossibly long, comprised of dozens upon dozens of rail cars, it shouldn't have even been *able* to stop so quickly. My feet had been rooted to the spot since I'd seen the collision, as if I was part of the street now, an immovable object that vehicles would have to drive around once the level crossing was operational again.

"You saw all this then?" I heard. I tried to look over my right shoul-der, but the persisting neck pain prevented me from going too far. I instead turned left almost three-hundred and sixty degrees to see the person standing beside me. It was Sergeant Digby, a member of the Black Bridge police department. As it was Sunday, the police station was actually closed, so his presence initially surprised me.

In small towns around the UK there exist a number of police stations that operate part-time. To anyone that lives in a densely populated area it must seem like sheer madness, but here it is totally normal. Across the Lake District you are unlikely to find many stations open past noon on a Saturday, it just isn't a place where a lot happens. Digby was wearing a fluorescent yellow rain jacket with 'Police' written across the back in enormous letters.

He also had on the iconic black hat of an English policeman, as if we needed any further clues as to his profession.

"Yeah, I was just about to cross to head to the shop and there was a car on the tracks," I began, watching him stroke at his beard like he was really listening. "It just slowed down and then nudged it down the embankment."

"Hmm, well typically a car on the tracks like this leads me to think that someone was looking for a way to end their own life. It's sad but true," Digby nodded. "I'll make a few calls, see if we can get this track approved for service and have this train on its way."

"And the car?"

"Oh, I'll get that towed away too. Probably call in the morgue people, that man is dead as a doornail!"

With that, Digby walked toward the trembling train driver and began to ask questions. Why was Digby even here? How did he know to get to this so fast in full uniform? The station was closed today, we all knew that.

"Never misses a chance to get in on the action," a familiar voice spoke. It was Police Constable James Webster, my ex-boyfriend. He wasn't in uniform, but rather a pair of running shorts and a long sleeve jersey that was clinging to his muscular physique. He had been out running early on a Sunday morning, that was apparently the kind of guy he was now.

I hadn't spoken a word to James since I'd come back to town, and looking at him now there was a moment of tranquility that briefly convinced me that no time had passed since our last conversation. Looking at him now I could be tricked into thinking we were eighteen again.

"Hi," I said, barely blinking.

"Did you see the whole thing?" he asked, not acknowledging my lame greeting. I nodded. "Odd that the train didn't pulverize it, don't you think?"

"Yeah, it was going so fast and then suddenly it wasn't," I said. His golden hair was slightly sweaty around his forehead and his cheeks were flush from exercise. "Do you need a statement?"

"Once the rail authorities show up they might appreciate a witness account, but it seems pretty obvious what happened here – car on the wrong side of the barrier when a freight train was roaring through. Are you planning on leaving town anytime soon?"

"No, why? Am I a suspect?"

"A suspect in a train crash?" he laughed. "Unless you somehow parked that Bentley there yourself and then pushed the train from behind until it hit the car, then no, you're not a suspect. I was just asking out of curiosity."

"Oh," I said, feeling myself blush slightly. "I'm sticking around for the foreseeable future."

"Good to know," he grinned. Somewhere in my heart the years apart from him had never happened. He looked happy, his blue eyes bright and his whole demeanor seemed lighter, as if he didn't have a single thing weighing him down. A thought hit me that maybe I'd never seen him like this before because our relationship had been holding him back. He was happy now because he was with someone else.

"When will they figure out cause of death?" I asked.

"There's a giant train shaped dent in the side of that car, so..."

"Yeah, but he was slumped in the passenger seat *before* the train showed up," I said.

"He? Do you know the victim?"

"I recognize the car. It belongs to one of the guys from Diversity

Capital, Hugh— I mean, Lionel Bassett," I replied. I had flirted with one guy since I'd moved back to this town, and he'd turned out to be evil, and now dead. It was hard not to take that personally.

"Come with me," James said. I trotted along behind him like an obedient dog, stepping onto the gravel area between the now-risen barrier and the edge of the train track, walking down to the car that was upside down on the grass a few feet to our left. "Actually, this is probably not something I should be doing."

"What do you mean?"

"Taking a civilian to a crime scene. There's a dead man in there."

"How do you know he's dead? I've been here the entire time and as far as I'm aware, no one has been close enough to take his pulse. The driver jumped out of the train and started screaming about having killed him, but he might not be dead!"

"Fair point," James nodded. He crouched down to peer through the driver's window with me a few feet behind him. I didn't need to get any closer, I could see plenty from here.

Lionel Basset *was* dead. His shirt was torn, his skin grey and mottled. There was a mark on his neck, something slightly darker than his paling complexion. He was now crumpled into a strange position against the roof above the driver's seat, despite having been sat on the passenger's side when I'd seen him. It had only been the back of his head that I'd spotted before the train hit, but I *knew* he hadn't been behind the wheel.

The dent from the train was on the driver's side, the doors were scratched and scuffed, the metal crumpled and the windows smashed. There was glass everywhere. I first noticed the glass when I knelt down to get a closer look at the damage.

I pressed my palm into the grass and winced as a small shard of glass imbedded itself into my skin. James turned to me in an instant, taking my hand in his and holding it close to his eye to inspect the injury.

It was one piece of glass, not particularly large, and James pulled it out swiftly and pressed a tissue to the wound to stem any bleeding. He must have had a tissue in his pocket, I was trying not to look right at the wound in case the sight of blood caused me to faint and embarrass myself.

I felt a heat flare up over my entire body. Twenty minutes ago we were deep into our years long no-communication streak, now here we were standing on the grass in Black Bridge with our hands clasped together.

"Thank you," I said, not daring to look him in the eye.

"No problem."

"Shame about that car, eh?" Digby hollered and strutted over to us in his bright yellow coat.

"Excuse me, Sir?" James said, releasing his grip on my hand now that we were in company.

"A Bentley, of all things. Such a beautiful car, British made and slick as a pin," he sighed. I hadn't heard the phrase 'slick as a pin' before, I was quite certain he had meant to say, 'slick as a whistle', but now wasn't the time to be prodding a Sergeant on his day off, even if he was in full uniform.

"Yes, and the dead man inside it is also quite unfortunate," James added.

"It goes without saying, Webster! I've called the rail authorities and let them know that one of their drivers has just killed a man in a Bentley, they wanted to know the year it was made you know, such a loss," Digby tutted.

"The year the *car* was made, or the year the *man* was born. The man inside the car, the one that is now dead," I huffed.

"Oh, well these things happen, Elizabeth. I understand it can be quite upsetting for the faint of heart to see something like this, but I assure you we will have all this cleared away soon enough and you can get on with buying those flowers."

"I wasn't trying to buy flowers," I said, engaging with the lunacy for some reason, "and I don't think the train killed him."

"The man was parked on a train track and a train hit the car, now he's dead. It doesn't take a genius to figure out what happened here," Digby snorted, laughing in such a way that air erupted from both nostrils. *Urgh.*

"Clearly…" I muttered under my breath.

"Sir, I have a few more things to ask of Ms. Sutton before she carries on with her day, but it might be worth calling the rail authority again and having them send one of their teams down," James said.

"No need, Webster. It's all done and dusted as far as I'm concerned." Digby marched back toward the barrier and began making loud announcements to the remaining crowd that there was *'nothing to see here'* and that everyone should *'return to their homes and pop the kettle on'*.

"Is he serious?" I said, my eyes wide in amazement.

"As a heart attack, unfortunately."

We shared a moment of silence, looking at our shoes rather than each other or the upturned car. I looked back at Lionel. I had attended a few crime scenes in London, I'd been sent off to handle anything that involved a dead body but not salacious details. If there was a huge story attached to a murder then I would be shoved aside by the bigger-named reporters, but if someone was pulled out of the Thames river after a drunken stumble then it fell to me to show up and take notes.

In my experience with the gruesome I had learned that often a dead person will not look dead straight away. A conversation with a medical professional taught me that it takes between fifteen to twenty-five minutes for a body to turn blue, and then over the proceeding few hours, livor mortis will kick in.

Livor mortis was described to me as 'the settling of blood due to gravity', and I had felt queasy enough to need to sit down as the doctor had explained it. I'd seen a man that had collapsed and died in the high street, a lowly enough incident for the editor of the newspaper to send me to deal with. The dead man had died several hours before he was found, and the back of his legs, arms and torso had turned deep purple.

Lionel Bassett had tumbled when the car had flipped. He was no longer in a seated position, but crumpled up against the inside of the roof.

"Can you take off his shoes?" I asked.

"Excuse me?" James almost chuckled.

"His blood might have pooled in his feet, it might give us a time of death."

"Since when did you know about these things?"

"I'm smarter than I look," I offered, looking at him with a serious expression that let him know that if he didn't take Lionel's shoes off, that I would do it. Reluctantly, he squatted down and carefully tugged at the dead man's footwear. There was some mud in the tread, more than I'd first noticed.

It was a dress shoe, part of the smart outfit he had worn to the town hall meeting the night before, and paired with long dress socks that extended up past the ankle. His shoes were *very* dirty.

"Sock too?" James groaned.

"Yes please!"

"I don't really want to be getting my DNA all over this man's clothes," he protested.

I reached into my coat pocket and pulled out the small plastic bag I'd brought to carry home my muscle-ache cream and any snacks that might have accompanied it. I passed the bag over and James pulled it over his hand as an impromptu glove, pulling the sock down to reveal the purple staining on the foot and ankle.

"Oh my word," James gasped. He may be a police officer, but Black Bridge isn't the type of place where these things happen. A train hitting a car? Unheard of. I doubted James had ever even seen a dead body, let alone the various stages of a body after death and what they all mean. "What am I looking at, Liz?"

"To put it bluntly, this man has been dead for hours," I replied. James stood up and regarded me suspiciously. "The train didn't kill him, something else did. He wasn't in the driver's seat, I saw the car before the train came and he was definitely sitting on the passenger side. That has to mean that someone else drove the car onto the tracks then left, probably the same person that killed him."

He squinted his eyes, his brow tensed. This was the way his face contorted when he was letting an idea percolate. In the years apart it seemed that there was still plenty that I knew about him. He took a deep breath and nodded slightly, as if in agreement with a conclusion he had silently come to.

"I'll check with the Sergeant, see how long it should take for the morgue people to get here. You probably don't need to stay now, I mean, it's probably best if the police take over the scene," he said. *Oh.* My lips parted, braced to plead my case about staying until I knew what was happening. If I hadn't been here, then they would have dismissed the whole mess as a train accident.

As much as I could recognize the signs that James was mulling something over, he could still identify when I was about to fly off the handle.

"Thanks," he said, catching me off guard. "If you hadn't been here to see all of this happen then we wouldn't have a full picture." His acknowledgement of my contributions was something at least, maybe I didn't need to start an argument with— "I guess moving all the way to London was worth it after all."

There it was. The topic that neither of us had brought up yet, the colossal elephant in the room. I had broken up our relationship and disappeared to the capital city on a whim to follow my dream career, he had been unwilling to follow me and now I was back after the job had fallen apart. I had known that *I* was still hung up on the whole mess, but now I knew he was too.

"I went there to become a journalist," I said. "I was trying to make something of myself."

"And how did that pan out for you?"

"Don't take that tone with me. I'm back in this town because it all collapsed around me, and you think *now* is the best time to take cheap shots?"

"You'll be back out of here the first chance you get and you know it," James yelled. "This whole town was never enough for you, *I* was never enough. You wanted me to come with you but we both know that you would have dropped me like a stone if something better came along. You always have your sights set on the next great thing and if that meant throwing us away then so be it, right? I was disposable, you made that perfectly clear."

My mouth hung open, watching us replay the last time we'd spoken face to face. Our grand love affair had gone up in flames as we yelled at each other on the train platform not thirty feet away from where we were both currently stood. He had begged me to stay, but I got on the train anyway.

What was my next move? Do I stand here and tell him that leaving him on that platform was the biggest regret of my life? Should I confess to how many times I've fantasized about a world where I *didn't* get on the train and how we would be married by now? What if I told him that those feelings I had all those years ago never went away?

No. I wasn't mature enough to be so brutally honest with him. Now felt like a fine time for a dramatic exit and a sassy one-liner. "You can keep the plastic bag!" I sassed, turning cautiously to avoid hurting my neck again and walking away. *You can keep the plastic bag?* Not my best work, but it would have to do.

You don't turn back after you drop your line, you keep walking until you are comfortably out of sight. Those are the rules. I marched back along the tracks, walked around the train that was obviously still stopped in place and on towards the only grocery store in Black Bridge open at this time on a Sunday morning.

Sergeant Digby had done a fine job of shooing away spectators on one side of the tracks, but on the other there was a sizeable crowd. Among them were a group of men in their early seventies that I recognized as the founding members of the Black Bridge Trainspotting Society. Despite the hour, here they were. Each of them had their own digital cameras, some fitted with pricey looking lenses, and were enthusiastically taking pictures of the train in front of them.

"Morning guys, big day for you, huh?" I offered.

"Oh, Lizzie, that is a British Rail Class 66. You rarely get to see them up close like this, especially here. They are normally racing past our sleepy little town and now I can see the delightful details of the axles, look at the metal work!" George chimed. George was the self-proclaimed president of the society, and no one questioned his authority on account of his encyclopedic knowledge of train engines.

"Oh she's a beauty!" I smiled.

"You know, I've never heard a sound like it before," he replied, turning to me and taking his eyes off the train for a moment. "A train of that size should have a braking distance of around six-hundred feet. The sun has only just started to come up, meaning that when the train came it couldn't have seen the car until it was much closer."

"What are you saying?"

"I just don't think the train had the time to slow down after the driver was able to spot it, I only heard the screeching of brakes for a few seconds before it stopped. The train shouldn't have been able to stop, but it did! Weird, that's all."

George turned his attention back to the train and I followed his eye line, staring at the stationary engine and wondering if what he'd just said was true.

7

"You need to start from the beginning because you are literally killing me," Kari gasped, slumping down onto my grandmother's sofa and almost spilling her coffee. I had in fact located the easy-cook pastries and the smell of buttery, baked goods was wafting through the house to join the scent of coffee in the living room.

Once I had gotten home, warily crossing the tracks to see if James was still there – he was, and I'd just sprinted across hoping he hadn't spotted me – I'd let myself back into the house and called Kari.

"I'm. Dropping. *Everything,*" she'd announced, heavy pauses between each word to indicate the severity of the situation. There had been just enough time to shower and apply a generous layer of muscle heat cream to my aching neck before she had been pounding on the door.

No one thrived on my personal drama like Kari did. When I'd been in London, she'd actually been back in the states with family. She would be sending me photos of huge seafood platters from Maryland and I would show her a picture of the lowly packed-lunch I'd brough to the office for myself.

It was her sense of adventure and extroverted personality that made me go for the internship in the first place. Not that I could ever admit that to her, if she knew that our friendship had played a part in the breakdown of my relationship with James then she would be beside herself. Obviously, the break-up wasn't her fault. That was all me.

I'd applied for the job in London because I wanted my own exciting life, and I naively thought that James' reaction would have been to pack a bag and jump on the train with me. He had deep ties to this place, he was happy here in a way that I never was. I always felt like the big fish in the small pond, wanting something more, something better.

I guess James had a point, if 'happy' was always somewhere else than I would never be satisfied with where I was. This was no time for deep, philosophical quandaries, Kari was desperate for juicy details about my reunion with James and she could barely contain herself.

"I did mention on the phone that I saw a dead guy today, right?" I said, laughing at the wild look in her eyes that betrayed her excitement.

"Yeah, I know. I'm sure it's super sad and super, you know, gross and everything. You can tell me all about that part later, you know what I'm here for!"

"Alright, well he showed up behind me in his running gear and—"

"Sweaty?" she interrupted. I nodded. "Oh man, his running route goes passed my house and I catch him sometimes as he races along the street. That man has thighs that could crush a watermelon…"

"Kari?!"

"Look, your ex-boyfriend is a prime cut of meat. I know I shouldn't objectify him, but those hams are something else!"

"He's dating someone you know," I reminded her.

"Victoria Cressley? She has all the personality of a bean sprout and a really nasty attitude about you in particular," Kari huffed.

"Me? What have I done?"

"Are you serious? You are *the girl* that got away. James was moping around this village for an upsettingly long time after you took off to London, everyone knows it. I wasn't even in Black Bridge and I heard about it," she explained. "You were the big super star journalist that made it out of this tiny place and took off for fame and fortune, people talked about you like you'd gone to the moon!"

"That's ridiculous."

"Is it? Your parents were telling every single person in that restaurant that their daughter was a hot-shot reporter in the city. Before you grandmother left she was ordering copies of the paper you worked for and scrapbooking any articles that had your name attached to them. Ernie at the store even started stocking that paper to sell, and it did! It would fly off the shelves, Liz."

"I didn't know anyone was doing that," I replied.

"Of course you didn't, because after you left you didn't come back until you *had* to."

Eesh, that one stung.

"I was busy, I just—"

"If London had worked out we wouldn't have seen you again, we both know it's true. When you called your mom and said you were coming home she told everyone not to mention London so that you wouldn't be too upset."

"She did what? That's so embarrassing," I groaned.

"She cares, not that she shows it to your face all that much, but she does. Victoria and James got together almost about eight months ago, when news got out that you were coming home I think James started acting a little differently. I mean, it was around then that he started running every morning. I think he was trying to get in shape before you got back."

"Don't be ridiculous," I scoffed.

"You don't think Vic could sense a shift in the air? If I was her I'd probably have it out for you, too," she shrugged.

"James and I got into a massive argument on the tracks this morning. He screamed at me about London, he was wild. I don't think Vic has anything to worry about," I replied.

"Oh really? Because what I just heard is that your ex-boyfriend is still so passionate about how your relationship ended that he is willing to fight with you about it."

"That sounds like the toxic nonsense people used to teach little girls, '*he's only pulling your hair because he likes you*'," I mocked.

"I'm right, I just know I am. Are those pastries ready yet because I ran here before I ate breakfast and I'm starving," Kari said, thus ending the conversation on her terms.

I was happy to stop talking about it. I went into the kitchen and there was still one minute left on the oven timer so I leaned against the counter and watched the pastries turn a rich, golden brown. I cleared my mind of all thoughts that weren't related to what I was about to eat, distraction was going to be the key to getting through the rest of the day after the interaction with J— nope, not even going to think about his name. *Pastries.*

It wasn't long after we'd finished eating that my mother called around to the house with an ungracious pounding of her fists against the front door. It was reminiscent of the force with which debt collectors would announce their arrival before they took away all your valuables.

"Mom?" I answered as I opened the door. "Where's the fire?"

"I need you to come into work today. I *know* it's your day off and you are going to be salty about it, but everyone is buzzing around town because of the train incident this morning and a huge group of people have shown up to investigate the crash so they will need feeding!"

"You can't be serious," I sulked.

"Elizabeth Aurelia Sutton," she barked. *Oh boy, full name.* "There is a swarm of hungry people that will descend upon us in a matter of hours and I am asking, sincerely, for you to help. Are you going to say no to my face?"

If emotional manipulation was a sport, then my mother would be an Olympic gold medalist. We all know the 'full name' tactic from a parent, it's nothing new, but she'd thrown in the word 'sincerely' and was now hunched over slightly to create the illusion that she was suddenly some frail, older lady that couldn't cope without my assistance.

"Fine," I moaned. It wasn't like I actually had any plans, but that had sort of been the whole point. It was a day to do absolutely nothing other than eat, watch a little TV, maybe fire up my PS5 and blast some zombies with a double barrel shotgun. You know, relaxing Sunday stuff.

"I can pop in and grab some lunch later," Kari chimed, "maybe catch you on your break and we can chat some more!" She winked at me as she skipped through the doorway with a croissant in one hand and her phone in the other. "Bye!"

"Do you want to wait inside while I get dressed? I washed my uniform after the ketchup incident and—"

"The ketchup explosion that happened when you were flirting with that devil man from that hedge fund?" she interrupted.

"I didn't know he was an investment guy at the time. He's dead by the way, so you might not want to go around town cursing him out," I explained.

"Dead? I suppose he caused that mess on the train tracks then."

"How have you found a way to blame a dead man for that? His car was on the— you know what, I'm just going to get dressed and you can just…" I gestured to the living room and she stepped into the house.

"It's a mess in here, Elizabeth. You really ought to be taking care of the place, your grandmother is on her way back from Greece and she'll probably want to come in to see her house."

"Wait, what?"

"I know it's *your* place now, but she still technically owns it and you do have two bedrooms upstairs so it's not as if you can't share. I don't know how long she is planning to be back for, but she said after speaking with you she got the sense you needed some matriarchal guidance. I thought that was slightly rude given that *I* am your mother and obviously giving you more than enough attention but—"

"She said she spoke to me?" I said, cutting her off. "I didn't speak to her, what is she talking about?"

"Your grandmother was very clear, she spoke to you last night and you were giving off a weird energy – her words – so she decided to get off the cruise at the next port and find her way to a plane to get back here. I don't know what you've said to her to get her to cut a cruise short, Elizabeth, but she was ranting about Diversity Capital coming to take over the fields around town. I was planning to tell her myself, but I was waiting for the right time…"

"She didn't call, we haven't spoken on the phone. I had a dream and… I mean maybe I spoke to her on the phone and then dreamt about it. I don't remember a phone call…"

"She mentioned that you should dust the light fitting in the living room, those were her parting words before she hung up."

I thought back to the dream I'd had about floating up off the sofa and hovering at ceiling height, looking down at the furniture. I'd seen the dust myself, but that had all been a dream.

I left the room and scurried up the stairs to get ready for my last-minute shift at the restaurant. Maybe a day of work making food for my fellow Black Bridge residents would take my mind off the James stuff, the dead man on the tracks and the bizarre conversation with my grandmother.

The queue was already out the door when I had arrived. My father was behind the cash register ringing up orders and a heavily pregnant cousin of mine was carrying a tray of drinks to a table full of out-of-towners that I assumed were here to investigate the train crash.

"Let me take that," I insisted, taking the tray with both hands and casting a disparaging look at my parents. Of all the people in the family to drag out of bed on a Sunday morning to help with the restaurant, they'd chosen the person who should be getting the most sleep.

"Deanna is on her way, too!" my mother hollered at me. "But Marla offered to help for half an hour until I tracked down a more suitable replacement."

"I'm more than happy to help," Marla said, sounding breathless from the short walk with the drinks.

"You need to escort her home, and maybe have a word with yourself on the way," I snarled at my parents. My father removed his apron, skipped over to Marla's side and helped her out of the door to the pavement that lead back to the center of the village where she lived.

"Here you go," I said, turning to the customers and lowering the tray of coffees. There were three men, each with a face more saturnine than the last, and one woman that was smiling at me.

"Thank you," the woman said, distributing the beverages among her grumpy colleagues.

"Are you here because of the train?" I asked.

"Yes, we are part of the team inspecting the level crossing to make sure it is safe before the track is put back into operation. The car's been moved now so the freight train could—"

"You're not supposed to tell the public stuff about the train," the man sat next to her grunted. I don't know if they had all had a really rough morning, or if they were just curmudgeons, but this one spoke in a monotone drawl like he was three whiskeys deep and tired.

"Sorry, I'm still new to the job. It hasn't beaten me down yet, not like..." her eyes roamed to the three men at the table and I nodded in acknowledgment.

"Elizabeth," my mother called from the counter. "These sandwiches won't make themselves!"

"Yeah, and you won't make them either," I muttered under my breath.

"Elizabeth Sutton?" the woman in front of me asked.

"Yeah, how did you..."

"I have you down as a witness to the incident on the tracks this morning. It would be beneficial to get an official statement from you, I know the police said they planned to catch you later today as well so I know you'll be busy." *Great.*

"Well I'm here until the place closes," I grimaced. "But we shut earlier on a Sunday so if you come back at around three o'clock I'll be cleaning up."

"Perfect!" she smiled. She was infinitely cheerier than the men at her table, they didn't even look up as the conversation played out.

When Deanna showed up, the two of us worked together like we had as teenagers when this was our only source of income. Now, however, we weren't being paid. This was another example of my mother's expert emotional manipulation skills. Somehow she had convinced two grown women, on a Sunday, to come into work for free.

While we sliced bread, spread mayonnaise, melted cheese and seasoned salads, my mother sat on her stool typing in prices to the cash register screen and taking payments. She rarely got stuck in with the messy side of the job. When my dad got back from taking Marla home, he took food to tables and cleaned up after messy customers.

In high school, Deanna and me would work with the radio on just a little too loud, playing silly games with each other to keep the days interesting. More often than not the games involved trying to sing to the customers instead of speaking, or only replying in song titles as they ordered.

When Deanna greeted an angry looking blonde with the words "Hello, is it me you're looking for?" I almost fell over laughing. I ducked down behind the counter to hide my face until I was able to calm down, but found that the mood soured quickly when the customer called out my name.

"I know you're down there, Liz," she hissed. I stood up, my expression now more neutral even though a smirk threatened to pull at my lips.

"Hello," I said, scanning her face for something I might recognize. Then it hit me. This was the face of a woman who had been printed next to a review of five model train engines for a local magazine last month: Victoria Cressley. "How are you?" I offered.

"I think you know *exactly* how I am," she snarled. I looked over at Deanna who was trying to mouth the words 'red flag' at me, but it was too late. "James said he bumped into you this morning, that's awfully convenient don't you think."

"We saw each other but—"

"Everyone in town knows his running route by now, and there you are standing right in the middle of it, you were waiting for him weren't you." It wasn't a question; it was an accusation and I was almost so amazed by how ridiculous it sounded that I couldn't form a response. "Aren't you going to say anything?"

"I was walking from my house to the little grocery store across the tracks to get something to help with neck ache, I witnessed a train crash and was still standing there with James showed up. I have no idea what his 'running route' is, so to think I was lying in wait like some sort of—"

"Predator?" she cut me off.

"We spoke about the train thing, that's it," I lied. There was no use bringing up the London argument when she was already annoyed with me. In an ideal world she would take note of the fact that she was in a public place and lower her voice, but she didn't seem interested in keeping our business private.

"Funny, he had blood on his shirt."

"A man was killed, there was a dead body there, that doesn't seem that weird to me," I replied.

"Oh Elizabeth, don't talk about dead people near the food," my mother scolded. I shot her a look. Did she think that the lettuce would spoil if I spoke of unsavory matters?

"Well I heard that you cut yourself on a piece of glass and he helped you clean it up."

"Are you spying on me?"

"So it's true? You thought you could just trick him into holding your hand by slicing it up a little on a few shards of smashed up window!" Her voice was loud enough now that it had totally cut through the conversations of other customers, and everyone had fallen silent to listen to our discussion play out.

I narrowed my eyes at her, wishing that I wasn't wearing a food-stained apron so that I felt on equal footing for this confrontation. "You're out of your mind," I said. "I'm not standing here and explaining myself to you. I think you should leave."

I didn't shout, but my tone let her know that I was serious. She looked around the room as if searching for people to support her, and found a sea of faces turning away to avoid eye contact. Deanna folded her arms and stepped beside me.

"Now," Deanna added. Victoria stomped her heeled foot and turned for the door, leaving in a fluster. "That's probably the start of a whole heap of mess."

My cousin was right. That wouldn't be the last I heard from Victoria.

8

My dad was mopping the floor around me and whistling a happy tune as he did so. Deanna had been put in charge of storing all the fresh food into airtight containers and refrigerating them and my mother, well she'd announced five minutes before the restaurant closed that she needed to leave to collect my grandmother from the airport.

I was sitting across from the friendly woman that I'd served earlier as she worked her way through a list of questions about the incident. She'd already asked me to write down my version of events and it felt like I'd been handed a long-form essay question with the teacher lurking over my shoulder, tapping their foot for me to hurry up.

My hand had seized up with a cramp as I tried to scribble down my testimony quickly and as I massaged my palm she continued with her enquiry.

"You say it was dark at the time of the collision."

"Was that a question?" I asked.

"Yes, was it dark?"

"Mostly, the sun came up about fifteen minutes later, or twenty... I didn't look at my watch or anything," I stuttered.

"Did you witness the victim drinking or taking illicit substances at any point over the previous twenty-four hours?"

"I barely knew the guy, he came in here for a sandwich, I saw him parked on double-yellow lines yesterday morning and then at the town hall he—"

"Sorry, did you just say you saw him parked illegally *yesterday* morning?" she pushed.

"Yeah, outside the coffee shop at the far end of the street by my house."

"So he had a history of disregarding the law with regards to parking, interesting," she said, noting it down.

"Whoa, that seems like a bit of a stretch. Plenty of people park illegally if they are running in to grab a coffee, that's completely different from parking on a train track," I countered. I had been suckered in by a friendly face, but now I see she was manipulating the facts to make Lionel look like he'd brought this on himself.

"I heard that he was booed off stage at the town hall meeting last night, does he strike you as the type of man that would like a hard drink after a tough day at work?"

"It's not my place to say," I hissed.

"From what I can gather, Ms. Sutton, you are under the impression that Lionel Basset was deceased prior to the train collision. That is consistent with our findings that the National Rail is not responsible for his death. As far as I am concerned, this is a case for the local police to clean up and we get to wash our hands of it, thanks for your help."

"Is that it?" I complained.

"I am part of a team looking into train safety, I have to sign off that the driver was unable to avoid the collision, and it will be noted that the man in the car was already dead. The medical people at the morgue agree that the timeline of death doesn't quite match up with the train schedule, so it's no longer my problem."

"You waited around Black Bridge all afternoon just to declare that this is a mess for someone else to fix, don't you care what happened to this man?"

"Truthfully, no I don't. Have a great day!" She scooped up her files, shoved them back into a large bag and headed out the door.

"Did you hear that?" I yelled to my dad. He had continued whistling throughout the conversation and I wondered how much he'd overheard.

"I sure did, you know those business types are only ever out to defend themselves. They have no sense of community, I didn't expect anything else," he replied.

"Speaking of community," Kari said, making her presence known.

"I have never heard anyone come through that door so quietly, that was terrifying," I laughed.

"Well I forgot to come over on your break."

"Oh, I didn't get a break today, did I dad?"

"Don't look at me! A freight train parked in the center of town brought a lot of nosy tourists that wanted to get their hands on high quality food at a reasonable price, we needed to work non-stop!" Dad smiled.

"We don't need a sales pitch, dad."

"I came by to say that I thought we should have a cookout!" Kari said, trying to pull focus back in her direction.

"A what?"

"A cookout, what do you call it? Oh, like a BBQ but it's not in your back yard, garden, whatever. We take a bunch of stuff to build a fire and go out to the fields to make dinner. We did it a bunch of times that one summer after high school exams, remember?"

"Yeah, vaguely," I replied, casting my mind back to over nine summers ago when we would do all sorts of zany stuff to keep us out of the house and away from the prying eyes of our parents. Those 'cookouts' – as Kari calls them – where part of one of the best summers we had in Black Bridge. James and I were dating then, the weather had stayed warm for weeks and it was the perfect way to say goodbye to our responsibility-free childhoods.

Of course I'd already been working at the restaurant by then, but my wages went on things like dresses and cheap beer at that one place that didn't check our ID. There was only really one college close enough for us all to go to, and we had all chosen our courses. There was very little overlap, Ed was in my English Literature class but that was it.

James had gone to pursue the qualifications needed to get into the police training academy, everyone else in our friendship circle had done a myriad of things such as math, accounting, law, politics and art. Here we were all these years later, still in the same town.

"I know it rained this weekend already, but the grass out there has been in the sun all afternoon so it's probably dry by now," Kari said, elevator pitching her social gathering idea. "If you give me the green light then you know everyone else will agree to it to."

"Fine, what time are you thinking?" I said, happy that Kari was on this side of the Atlantic because she always arranged the fun stuff around here.

"I'm thinking five, that field by the stream, you know the one?"

"Yep!"

"Okay, I have to go and find firewood, matches, meat, burgers, cheese…" she was listing off groceries as she left the restaurant and disappeared up the road.

"Well that's my night sorted," I smiled, turning to Deanna who was giving me *the look*. "You are obviously invited too!"

"Lizzie, she already texted everybody," Deanna laughed. "You just didn't get the message because you were talking to that psycho from the national rail."

"What?"

"Yeah, Kari is making it like a town-wide invitation for everyone under thirty-five."

"She just said that I needed to give the green light!"

"She was playing you," Deanna grinned. "It sounds like it's going to be pretty epic though, so it's good to have you on board."

Maybe everyone I knew was good at emotional manipulation then, not just my mother.

"Your grandmother wanted to see you, Lizzie," my dad added. "What time will your little party be over?"

"I have no idea, dad."

"Well make sure to have your phone nearby for when your mother calls to say she's back in town. If you don't answer then I'm the one that bears the brunt of her foul mood!"

"Hey, you married her," I teased.

I had been put in charge of relishes. When I had messaged Kari to ask if she needed me to pick anything up for the cookout – or BBQ as everyone else would be calling it – she had suggested I grab a jar of caramelized red onion relish. I couldn't imagine a version of this event where anyone was carefully adding relishes to burgers and hotdogs; we were cooking meat in a field for crying out loud, it wasn't a sit-down meal.

I dutifully purchased it, though. I had a bag over my shoulder with a waterproof coat, relish, a bottle of water, painkillers and burn gel. My friends laughed at my cautiousness around fire, but I didn't see what was so bad about being prepared for the worst just in case. We were building a huge fire in the middle of a field, why wouldn't I bring burn gel? All it would take was for someone to trip over an errant shoelace or a branch and they could really hurt themselves! As you can imagine, I'm not always the most fun at parties.

The journey from my house to the field by the stream was maybe a ten-minute walk, but I could cut that down to eight if I sped up a little. I was already running late on account of it taking longer than usually to clean up the restaurant. Despite having a policy for customers to clear away their own trash, we would still always find wrappers, empty sugar packets and food scraps under the tables.

It would have been the tourists that made the mess, the locals wouldn't dare. My mother had a reputation in this town that meant people wouldn't flagrantly disregard her 'leave the place as you found it' sign in the window. She was firm, but fair. If you weren't her daughter that is.

Considering that she was the owner of a restaurant, one that also had a hot grill to serve up eggs and bacon, it was amazing how much respect she'd earned in this town. That sounds cruel, as if I'm suggesting that there's nothing noble about that as a job, but you have to remember that if she is ever *in* the restaurant, she is usually out back reading a magazine.

If she goes to those town meetings and voices an opinion, everyone else in the room begins to agree and back her up. People come to her with problems too, knocking on the door of her house and asking to speak to her in private. Sometimes people are upset and speak to her with a view of feeling better... and she actually helps them. It was nothing like my own experience with her. I felt like the rest of Black Bridge had a better relationship with my own mother than I did.

If I could afford a therapist, I was quite sure they'd tell me that my maternal issues were at the heart of most of my insecurities.

Kari had been right about the weather; the sun beating down on the fields for the bulk of the afternoon had dried out the rain and there was a warm breeze drifting through the air. As I approached the fence that bordered the field I could see the group gathered around Kari, she was on her knees trying to build a fire and not a single one of the people behind her seemed to be helping.

Because of where my house was in relation to the field, it was unlikely that any of the others had come this way. I would sometimes wander out of town and go on hour-long hikes through the greenery of the Lake District. It always amazed me how long I could walk out here without seeing another soul, I wouldn't even make it to the next town over in that time. Once you got beyond the built-up area of Black Bridge, you were out into the fields and hills, roaming through woodland and around marshes.

The sun may have dried up the grass, but the mud patch by the area of fence I was about to climb over still looked wet enough to stain my shoes. I was wearing white converse – why did I do this to myself? – so needed to plan my route carefully.

The tarmac of a road blended into a broad, muddy area and then the fence sprung up out of the depths of it. Hedges had grown around the fence in most other places, so the only clear part for me to climb over was right here, or another ten-minute walk down the road to the other corner of the field where everyone else had likely entered.

The mud had a tire track pressed into it, curving toward the fence but then stopping. Whoever had driven the car here must have reversed back away from the fence. Footprints in the mud beside the tire tracks suggested that someone had walked here recently, the sudden appearance of them suggesting someone had exited the car to walk around.

Something white and plastic caught my eyes. In that moment my curiosity outweighed my interest in keeping my converse clean, so I stepped into the mud and picked up what turned out to be a hotel swipe card. It was for 'The Belmont', a hotel on the outer edge of town that catered to tourists with a higher budget.

"Lizzie! Can you help me with this fire?!" Kari hollered. I slipped the hotel card into my bag and decided I could return it to The Belmont tomorrow. I began to climb over the fence and almost tripped over the wooden handle of a spade that was camouflaged against the dirt on the ground, before hurrying across the grass to get to the group.

"I thought you were in the Girl Scouts," I teased, crouching down beside Kari to stare into the dry logs that were still not on fire.

"I was! But this English weather is a joke and the wood here is wet even when it's not, do you know what I mean?" she complained. I didn't even have a chance to fully take note of everyone who had gathered so far, I had noticed a few of my inner circle of friends as I'd approached the group but more people joined, then more.

After ten minutes, and sixty-eight burned out matches, someone produced a pack of Firestarter cubes, gasoline-soaked bricks that burned slowly enough that the wood could catch. I had a slight grass stain on both knees, my forehead was a little sweaty now and my converse would never be the same.

Ed, Will and Owen had each stood back and watched the fire building go on without offering assistance, but now that it was roaring, they decided to take charge to cook the food. I was happy to let them, I didn't much fancy standing by the heat for much longer. Kari handed me a drink and I sat down on one of the dozen blankets that had been scattered in a huge circle.

Natasha, the third woman in our group of six friends, sat down beside me and clinked her beer bottle against my own. She was quiet, always had been. To engage her in conversation was difficult sometimes but she was clearly feeling bold today.

"I think I'm turning to the dark side," she announced.

"What are you talking about?" Kari laughed.

"Diversity Capital asked me a few days ago to design a website for the retail park they are planning to build and they have offered to pay double my usual rate," Nat replied. You might not think that someone so reserved could run a successful IT company by herself, but she does. Natasha started small with a team of one – herself – and now has a team of three or four.

"And you said yes!?" Kari screeched. She was scandalized, as was I.

"It's a lot of money!" Natasha countered.

"Alright, let's just take a breath here," I urged. "They haven't signed off on purchasing the land yet, so why would they be giving you a ton of money to make a website for something that might not even get built."

"Well I was told that the land has been sold already. Stephen Berry has already signed the contracts."

A hush fell over the small crowd that was close enough to hear. Now Natasha was holding court, confidently so, and no one dared to interrupt.

"The town hall was just a formality; it was supposed to be a way for the investors to win you all over but it obviously didn't work out so well. They figured that if they hired a local firm to design the website, made a point to be putting money into our community, that we might all change our minds about the green belt," she explained.

"Who else knows about that?" James asked. I felt my stomach tense, glancing up at the tall figure standing beside me. He wasn't alone. Victoria Cressley was right there next to him wearing a ridiculous pair of designer heels and a dress so tight I could almost see her organs.

"I don't know, but Councilor Berry was with them when they came to me. The guy that spoke from Diversity Capital, Lionel something, he was there too. He's the one who told me about how much they were willing to pay, my eyes nearly shot out of my head."

"Who else from your company was in that meeting?" James pressed.

"My whole team," Nat replied.

"What are you thinking, babe?" Victoria asked, making a point to wrap her arm around James' back and glaring at me to make sure I noticed.

"It's just interesting, that's all," he nodded. He was thinking it over, I could tell. Lionel was dead and he had secretly had the sale of the green belt approved unbeknownst to the people of this town. It basically meant that almost anyone in Black Bridge had a reason to want him gone, but who had the means and opportunity to actually kill him?

"Why don't you tell everyone about the contract *I* just signed with that clothing catalogue?" Victoria said, shaking James gently to get him out of his thoughts. "My face is going to be up in the stores of a major high street brand so we will probably have to move out to London or something soon because my career is taking off!"

"What?" James scoffed, laughing loudly enough to cause ire from his girlfriend. "I thought you were just invited to audition, did you sign something?"

"Well... no but my agent is confident that..." she stuttered.

"I'm not going to London," he asserted, wriggling out of her embrace and walking over to the cooler to get himself a drink. Despite the fact that her boyfriend was the one that had just caused a scene, she was staring at me with the rage of something that had decided it was all my fault.

Nat, Kari and I continued to talk about everything *but* the James situation until the sun went down, at which point one of the guys produced a glow in the dark frisbee and insisted we all jump up to play a giant game of fetch in the dark.

It wasn't supposed to be fetch, but as no one could really see the frisbee all that well until it landed it meant that we were mostly running around to pick it up before throwing it again.

With bellies full of burgers, ketchup laden hotdogs and drinks, none of us were at our athletic best. Ed threw the frisbee into the woodland area by mistake as he couldn't see where any of us were now that the fire was dying down and I volunteered to retrieve it. I was surprised to hear another pair of feet crunching through the undergrowth behind me.

"Lizzie," a voice said. It was James, I would recognize that silhouette anywhere.

"What are you doing?"

"I wanted to apologize for this morning. I said some things that I shouldn't have said, I got too heated with it but I know cooler heads prevail so I just wanted to check that we're okay."

"You meant what you said though, I know you did. It's fine for you to be mad with me, I wish you weren't obviously but..."

"I don't want to be," he blurted. I could see his face now only a foot away from my own, I could *feel* him closer to me.

"I knew you were a snake!" Victoria shrieked, shining a flashlight directly into my eyes so that I couldn't see a thing. "Dragging *my* boyfriend into the woods to try and steal him? I shouldn't have expected anything less!"

"Vic, nothing was happening, we were talking," James said, a defeated sigh escaping his lips as if he was tired of having this exact fight.

"Oh yeah? I suppose this conversation couldn't have happened in the middle of the field where everyone else is though, it just *had* to happen in the woods when you are alone?!"

"We are allowed to talk," I muttered.

"I warned you already to back off," Victoria hissed.

"You did *what?*" James gasped.

"Did you forget to mention the part where you came into my family's restaurant to yell at me in front of customers?" I smirked. Okay, I didn't want to be petty but if she wanted to drag me down into the dirt with her then fine.

"I'm going home," James huffed. "Lizzie, do you need a ride?"

"Hey, what about me?" Victoria wailed. She lifted her hands up to push me back, I could see the flashlight in her grasp as she reached for me and then suddenly a burst of energy seemed to explode from me and she fell over. No one saw what had happened because it was too dark, but I knew. It felt like a force stretched out of my body and pushed her to the ground.

What was happening?

—————

9

*N*eedless to say, I freaked out. Victoria snapped the heel on an expensive pair of shoes on her way down to the muddy ground and her skin-tight dress was ruined. Or so she claimed, I hadn't actually seen her. The flashlight she had been holding had waved about in every direction and I could just about make out the shape of James standing there staring at her, perhaps wondering if he should help her to her feet or not.

Kari offered to give me a ride home, which in fact just meant that a bunch of us walked home together. I had been left at my front door and waved my friends off as they continued on up the street to the next person's house.

I woke up with a pounding headache, something I attributed to not having drank enough water yesterday and rolled over in bed determined to source some. I grabbed a robe, wrapped it around my body and shuffled down the stairs, almost falling down the last five steps when a voice started talking at me from the living room sofa.

"What time do you call this?" my grandmother laughed. I grabbed onto the handrail to prevent falling to my untimely death and she continued to chuckle as she turned to see me.

"Why are you talking while facing the other way, like a Bond villain?" I complained, pulling myself back onto my feet and making my way down to the ground floor. "When did you even get here? How long have you been sat staring at the living room wall?"

"Your mother collected me from the airport and brought me straight here last night, you weren't around so I just took myself up to the guest bedroom and had a lie down, seems I slept right through!"

Something beside her was moving. I had thought it was a coat thrown haphazardly against the cushions, but quickly realized that it was a cat.

"Are you for real? You let a cat in here? What is happening?" I rushed over to nuzzle the cat behind its ear, astonished by the silky fur that coated it's tiny kitten body. "Where did you get a kitten?"

"It was mewing at your back door, Lizzie," my grandmother smiled. "It wanted to come in, it's chosen you!"

Her hippie attitude to letting a stray animal into her home had caught me off guard, but I had always wanted a pet cat so this could actually work out for the best. Then a thought struck me.

"It's so tiny, it's probably just wandered away from its family," I winced, imagining the poor thing stranded out behind my house and calling for me to let it into the warm.

"He's chosen you, Lizzie. This is all coming together much better than I thought it would," she grinned. "You know, I thought that it might have started when you moved back to Black Bridge, but it seems you're something of a late bloomer. Nothing to be embarrassed about of course, it just means there's a little catching up to do, that's all."

"What are you talking about?" I asked, but it seemed she didn't hear me as she was mid-monologue.

"I had words with your mother in the car, strong words. I told her it was cruel to have left you in the dark about all this for so long, I thought that leaving her to find her feet as a parent was the best thing to do and obviously *that* was a mistake. It takes a village, that's what they say! And this village, oh boy—"

"Am I part of this conversation or are you just talking to yourself?" I teased.

"Lizzie, it seems that your powers have started to kick in so it's time you participated in the coven of Black Bridge, and if you could also stop that horrid bunch of capitalist pigs from building a cheap Italian restaurant over the graves of our ancestors that would be just swell."

The presence of an adorable little kitten was obviously putting me in a better mood than usual, because I didn't immediately call for my parents to come and have grandma assessed for a head wound. "What powers would these be?" I said, playing along.

"Powers," she repeated. "You know what powers are, don't humor me Elizabeth Sutton, this is serious."

"Like, *magic* powers?" I scoffed.

"Exactly, the only kind worth having. I've heard a rumor that you slowed down a freight train all by yourself, and for a first attempt at using your strength I have to say I'm impressed. I don't think I could stop a feather from falling on my first try let alone six thousand pounds of steel. Shame that the chap in the car was already dead, but you thought you were saving a life and look what happened! Wait until your grandfather hears about this!"

"I didn't stop a train," I grimaced. "It hit the car, I don't know what you've been told, or *who* you've been speaking to but—"

"George from the trainspotting club," she chimed in, holding up a finger to indicate she didn't want me to continue speaking. "He told me that he heard the brakes screeching on the tracks and peered out of his bedroom window only to find you standing there with your eyes closed and a bright light bursting out from your chest. He actually called me you know!"

"Ahh, so that's how you know what's been going on around here. You had me thinking we'd spoken on the phone and I'd forgotten all about it," I laughed. "Did you and George cook this up together? I think he has a crush on you."

"Do I sound like I'm joking?" she said, her forehead tense as she regarded my response. "You are from a line of witches, a long line at that. I suppose you've heard the myths about this town being an old hideout for outlaws..."

She was referring to highwaymen, the thieves that would lurk behind trees and then ambush weary travelers at gun point to rob them of their riches. The Lake District has always been a popular place for tourists to visit, going back hundreds of years. Somehow Black Bridge went without a law enforcement presence for a long time, meaning that its residents were made up of criminals on the lam.

This was the story we all learned as kids, but it wasn't based on any truth. There was nowhere that thieves were safe from the police, it just didn't make any sense. I knew a few of the older folk around town would cling to the legend of our ancestry because it made the place sound more exciting, but really it was just a sleepy old town in the middle of nowhere that was the epicenter of tedium.

"Are you on the run from the cops?" I laughed.

"Enough," she snapped, pointing a finger at me and squinting her eyes. The blue of her eyes had only intensified with age. The snow white of her hair brighter now than it ever was, and her skin looking more youthful than I'd ever seen it. Had she gone on a cruise as a means to hide herself from us while she recovered from face lift surgery? Because it sure seemed like it.

At that moment my front door swung open and my mother stepped into the living room with a look of concern on her face.

"I hope I'm not too late, but I've decided I should tell her myself," she panted, breathless as if she had sprinted down the street to my house.

"You missed your chance, so I've done it," my grandmother replied.

"Hey, is there a gas leak in here? What are you both talking about?" I exclaimed, re-inserting myself into the conversation.

"Liz," my mom began. She rarely used my shortened name and I found myself shudder at the sound of it. "The women in our family, in your family, in the family that we—"

"Oh do get on with it!" grandma snapped.

"You're a witch!" mom shrieked. I raised an eyebrow at her and waited for the punchline. "I heard that you knocked Victoria Cressley off her feet last night and you didn't lay a finger on her, so clearly you are getting more attuned to your abilities."

"How did you hear about that?" I gasped.

"Kari told me," mom confessed.

"Why would my friend be calling you to tell you something so totally uninteresting? What's this all about?"

"When you left for your internship you walked away from a lot of things," mom began.

"And not just that drop dead gorgeous man of yours!" grandma added.

"Black Bridge is a powerful place, the very soil here makes it what it is. The green belt is important to us all because—"

"Are you kidding? You've cooked up some mad story with my grandmother just so you have another excuse to rant about the bloody green belt? I helped dad make his placard, I've written an article about the town hall meeting for the paper, what more do you want from me?" I blurted.

"The outlaws were witches, Lizzie," grandma added. "Not highwaymen, they weren't men at all, they were witches. Deep in the countryside became the only safe place to practice magic, so a group of them set up a village here and we never left. There is an old bridge that used to cross the river to get here from the South, it's dried up now of course – global warming isn't a joke – but *that* was the 'Black Bridge' that you had to cross.

"Once you walked over that bridge you were agreeing to a life that was *technically* illegal at the time. They actually legalized witchcraft in England in 1735 but the witches that lived here quite liked the fresh air at that point so they just stayed here."

"She thinks we're mad, this is exactly why I didn't tell her," my mom sighed.

"Just because something takes a while to understand, doesn't mean we avoid it forever," my grandmother huffed, standing up now to glare at me. She aimed her palms toward my body and ordered me to jump. Why I agreed to participate in the stupid charade I don't exactly know, but I bent my knees a little and propelled myself upwards. In the half-second that I was airborne I saw the room around me change, and when my feet landed on the ground again I was standing in the kitchen.

I had somehow travelled fifteen feet to my left mid-jump. I rushed back to the doorway to look at my mom and grandma in astonishment, the pair of them smiling back at me.

"Do you believe me now?" grandma asked.

"I was— how did you— I can't!" I gasped.

"You are a daughter of Black Bridge, a relative of the witches that the hunters never caught because they were too clever, too crafty. Their bones are buried out in the fields around this town and if those stupid developers storm in here with bulldozers and drills then they will destroy everything that makes this place so special!"

"Why is it suddenly all on my shoulders to fix this?" I complained, finally able to construct a sentence after several seconds of slack-jawed gawping.

"You shouldn't ask 'why me?', but rather 'why *not* me?'" my grandmother announced. "Now be a lamb and sort all of this out before our powers take a hit." With a snap of her fingers my grandmother disappeared, literally zapped out of the living room as if she had never been there, and I was left staring at the space that her body had just occupied.

I looked over at my mom, then back at the space.

"It's a lot to take in, I appreciate that," she shrugged. "But now you know so it's probably time to just make your peace with it and move on. I have been asked to cater a meeting for tomorrow afternoon so I was hoping you could come into the restaurant later to help me prepare for it, plenty of fresh cookies have been ordered so they can all be baked tonight."

"Excuse me? Did you not just watch your mother disappear into thin air like a wizard?" I shrieked.

"Like a *witch*, darling, and yes I did," mom nodded. "It's quite common not to tell witches about their powers until they are out of their teen years, can you imagine giving an eighteen year old those sorts of abilities? They'd become a menace!"

"How long have you known about all this?"

"About you being a witch? Or about witches in general?"

"I'll take answers for both, then I'm having a cold shower," I replied.

"Well I've known about witchcraft since I was about twelve or so, I think I crept down the stairs once to grab a glass of water and my parents were in the living room floating about like a couple of ghosts and they caught me looking. That's when they sat me down and had 'the talk', which was basically that if I promised not to tell a soul what I'd seen then they would show me how to use my own powers and—"

"Hold on, grandad was floating too? Is he a witch?"

"No, he just married one."

"Does everyone in the family know except me?" I asked.

"At this point, yes," she sighed. "I was almost hoping that you would just figure it all out for yourself and I wouldn't have to have an awkward conversation with you about it. Alas, I wasn't so lucky, but hey you slowed down a freight train all by yourself and Kari told me you knocked Victoria Cressley on her arse. You seem to be quite powerful already. With a little polish I think you'll be a great addition to the coven."

"Coven?"

"Yeah, our little gang. I suppose now that your grandmother is back in town that she is going to want to call a meeting, especially with these investors sniffing around the place, so I'll text you later with the details and you can come along to see what we do. It's not quite a debutante ball, Elizabeth, but wear something respectable, won't you? I don't want to see a t-shirt from a nineties sci-fi show and I would appreciate real shoes."

Before I could defend myself she had stormed out of the front door and onto the street. I saw her turn back to face me, click her fingers, and the door swung shut in her wake.

"Converse *are* real shoes, what does 'real shoes' even mean? They aren't pretending to be shoes, they fit the description of a shoe perfectly," I muttered.

"Are you really going to spend the day talking about shoes?" a voice asked. I looked around to find the source of the question, but I was alone.

"Who's there?" I said, quickly scanning the room to look for a suitable weapon if it turned out that someone had broken in.

"Am I invisible down here?" The only other living thing in this room was the dark-furred feline that was stretching out its legs along the back of my sofa.

"Did you just—?" I cut myself off, not willing to even entertain the idea that the cat was the one talking. I'd just seen my grandmother disappear, like some grand Penn and Teller stunt, and I couldn't cope with anything else outlandish so soon.

"I think I'm owed an apology," the cat replied. I didn't say a word in response, unable to take my eyes of the tiny mouth forming the shapes to speak. "First of all, I wasn't told that I was assigned to a beginner. This is embarrassing for me that I am now attached to someone so vastly incompetent that—"

"Whoa, that's rude!" I complained.

"Am I wrong? Did you not just find out about witchcraft in the last five minutes?" he mewed.

"Yes but—"

"Point proven! Look I'm sure you're good at something, but magic isn't it. When I heard that there was an opening for a member of the Sutton family, well I almost tripped over my own tail to sign up for that one. I just think that there was some false advertising and I think *technically* that's illegal."

"You want me to apologize for not knowing about magic even though it seems my entire family conspired against me to keep it a secret, is that what you're saying? You are a talking cat and you are choosing to use that gift to give me an attitude, how is this my life? I was out in the woods getting yelled at my ex-boyfriend's new girlfriend twelve hours ago and I thought *that* sucked. This is worse."

"There's no need to be mean!" the cat hissed.

"How am I the mean one here? I can't believe I'm talking to a cat, the last half hour has been—"

"How about this..." the cat interrupted. "If you give me some cream, or milk if that's all you have, then I will behave myself. It's not like I'm insensitive to the fact that you're new to all this, but I'm a cat so, you know, I put my interests first. It's in my DNA."

"I'll check the fridge," I sighed. I shuffled back into the kitchen that my grandmother had magically transported me to earlier. Had that all just happened? As a kid I always dreamed of having a talking pet, but this was something else.

I pulled open the fridge and stared in at the shelves, the cool air rolled over my bare feet. I reacted to what I'd just seen over and over, like the eb and flow of the tide. There would be half a second of relief as if I'd almost forgotten it all, then the memory would hit me again. My family had just told me, to my face, that I was a witch. They had proven that they had powers. A cat had spoken to me.

There was a small container of cream that I didn't remember having bought, but this was a morning to expect the unexpected. I tipped a little cream onto a saucer and turned to find the cat had already followed me into the room.

The black fur was quickly coated in white as the cat plunged its face into the snack, before lifting its head up to look at me.

"My name's Pepper by the way," he purred.

"Oh, do I not pick your name?" I muttered.

"Ha!" he scoffed. I had a mental list of dozens of cat names I'd earmarked for when I finally got a pet for myself, it hadn't been possible when I'd lived in London and I hadn't given it much thought since I got back to Black Bridge, but it seemed the choice had been made for me.

My phone buzzed in the pocket of my bathrobe and I pulled it out to read the message from my mom that she probably should have sent ten minutes ago.

'Elizabeth, the cat can talk, just so you know.'

10

The back yard of this house was small – 'quaint' is how my mother describes it – but it is better than nothing. When you've been sharing a home with a bunch of other underpaid twenty-somethings in London, you thank your lucky stars for a space like this. Up until now, though, I'd never spent much time out there, but Pepper had other ideas.

"You will need a cat door so that I can come and go as I see fit," he ordered.

"Are all kittens this bossy?" I teased.

"I think it's a perfectly reasonable request," he gasped. I laughed at the wide range of facial expressions he seemed capable of.

"Can't you magic your way outside?"

"I wouldn't waste my energy on something that you can do for me, that's sort of a cat mantra."

We had opened the back door and were staring out at the paved area and the yellowing grass beyond. The fences that separated this yard from the one's of each neighbor seemed to be splintering, and it looked like any plants in the flower beds had died the previous winter and their deaths had gone unnoticed.

"This is truly an embarrassing moment for you," Pepper sighed. "But with a little elbow grease we can turn this around."

"Why would it be embarrassing?" I asked.

"*This* is your outside space, why would you let it fall to ruin?"

"I get back from the restaurant and I watch TV or play video games. I don't want to be out here messing about in the dirt. I've got a career in journalism to resuscitate!"

"What an unusual list of excuses," he mewed, bounding down from the back door and sashaying along the patio towards the grass. "Come with me."

I was still in my bathrobe. Pepper had dived into a five-minute grooming routine after almost inhaling the cream I'd put down for him, and I still looked like I'd just rolled out of bed. I slipped my feet into a pair of crocs I had by the back door and followed Pepper to the flower bed he was now sat beside.

"What are those?" he almost shrieked, transfixed on my footwear.

"I have a compost thing at the far end of the garden for food scraps, these are the best shoes to throw onto my feet if I'm taking stuff outside when I'm cooking!"

"This situation is worse than I thought," he muttered to himself, although it was loud enough for me to hear and I suspected that was intentional.

"What are we doing out here?" I asked.

"Other than committing fashion crimes?" he mewed. I rolled my eyes. "We are going to try a little green magic to get the ball rolling. I hear that you've been stopping trains and shoving women to the floor and as wonderful as that is, let's start small."

"I didn't shove—" What was the point? Was I really going to stand outside my own home and argue with a cat? "What do you mean *green* magic?"

"Your garden is dying, this grass is yellow, there are weeds growing between those patio stones that have yet to be identified by botanists and you have a cat in your life with higher standards than this. We are going to start by reviving this rose bush."

My grandmother had a row of raised flower beds up against the fences on the left and right of the space. The one that Pepper was sat beside had a trellis attached to the back of it to act as a support frame for various vines at one end, and a rose bush at the other. It seemed that the rose bush had been woven carefully around the trellis at some point but was now pale and crispy in places.

"I want you to touch a finger to the plant, just above where it erupts from the soil," Pepper ordered.

"This is ridiculous," I groaned.

"You're ridiculous. Do what I say!" he sassed. This cat was going to be a handful, I could tell.

"You said if I gave you cream you would be nicer to me!" I countered.

"I don't recall using those exact words, but I take your point. I am trying to show you how to use your powers, I can appreciate that you are still skeptical about this whole thing so I am going to demonstrate to you that you are in fact a witch. Now touch the plant, *please*." He forced an unnatural grin and I did as was asked.

"What now?"

"Just think about giving this plant all the nourishment it would need to live, focus on that and try to clear your mind of everything else," Pepper said.

I resisted the urge to roll my eyes again and tried to follow the instructions. Okay, plants. Plants need water and... nitrogen? No that's not right, is it nitrates? There's something in soil isn't there, some weird chemical thing that they suck up through the roots. I know they need sunlight and they make oxygen, do they make it? Or convert it from something? High school science was a long time ago and I've done a million things since then.

"You're not concentrating!" Pepper sighed. "Picture how it will look if it's healthy."

Green. The leaves will be green.

Suddenly the stem closest to my hand plumped slightly, sharp thorns sprouted from it and one of the leaves turned from a pale yellow to a rich green. I gasped and pulled my hand away.

"Not bad for your first try," Pepper said, but his eyes suggested otherwise. "I guess the *whole* plant was too much to ask for, but it's a start."

"I just did that, that was... I can't believe it," I stuttered.

"Care to try again?" Pepper smiled. I repeated everything I'd just done, gazing in amazement at the flower buds bursting into vibrant reds, the petals velvety soft. The greenery spread upwards from the soil, winding its way around the trellis and finishing right at the top with one final rose. "Honestly, that was impressive. I don't say that often so I wouldn't get used to it."

"I should do that with everything here, right?" I said, giddy to do it again. The sensation in my hand was like tingling, as if I could feel energy transferring from me to the plant I had been touching.

"You should take a break, if you do too much at once you can burn out. The last thing you need is to run out of magic on your first day. Well, it's not your *first* day, but you haven't used any magic intentionally before so it's a bit different to instinctual, reflex magic, and don't even get me started on—"

"Run out? You can run out of it?" I asked.

"Yes. It's like a plane full of jet fuel, you know, it can only go so far with the fuel it has but if it runs out you can still land safely and—"

"What? If a plane runs out of fuel then it would fall out of the sky," I said.

"Hmm, yes that might be a bad analogy," he mused. "The point stands, you only get a certain amount of magic a day, over time that amount will increase and if you are ever in a real bind you have a reserve that is kept for emergency use. I don't know how it works, it just does. Oh, there's someone at the door!"

A second later I heard a knocking sound echoing through the house. I walked back across the patio, and stepped inside.

"Liz, are you here?" James called.

"Oh shoot," I groaned.

"Who is it?" Pepper asked.

"My ex-boyfriend."

"Oh, are you worried because you look like trash?" he said, adding a tilt to his fuzzy little head to convey pity.

"Well I am now!"

"Don't worry, this is one of the many ways in which I will make your life better," Pepper nodded.

"What do you mean?" I began to ask, but realizing that my crocs were now gone, replaced with a sophisticated pair of black heels. My robe fell away and disappeared like smoke, revealing a floral house dress that pinched in at the waist and gave me an hourglass figure that I didn't even know I had. My hair was no longer held up in a messy top-knot, but fell down in loose waves over my shoulders.

"You're welcome," Pepper purred.

"What just happened? Are you a genie?" I gasped.

"Better. I'm a familiar," he smiled. He bounced over to a sofa cushion and curled up in a fluffy ball. I could hear kitty snoring before I even made it to the door. I turned the handle and pulled, revealing Officer James Webster in all his uniformed glory. He was clearly struck by my appearance, and if I said it didn't make me feel good to see that expression on his face then I'd be lying. He used to look at me like that all the time.

"Liz, you—" he uttered.

"Hi," I smiled back. "How can I help you?"

"I was hoping to get a statement, maybe ask you a few questions," he said. "Could I come in?"

"Sure," I replied, stepping aside to make space for him to walk past me into the living room. He took a step, turning so that we were face to face for a brief moment, then stepped again. My heart thumped in my chest just like it had when he had held my hand on the train tracks to deal with the glass in my palm.

"Who's this little guy?" James cooed, spotting the sleeping kitten and reaching out a hand to pet him.

"Pepper, he's… new," I answered, "and super tired."

"Ah, I'll get a cuddle next time then," he laughed. *Next time?*

"You said you had questions?" I pressed, trying to gloss over the suggestion he'd made that he would be visiting me here again. It occurred to me that I hadn't given him my address, I wondered how he'd known where to find me.

"Yeah, it's erm… more of a curiosity thing at this point," he said.

"What do you mean?"

"Digby is not under the impression that anything suspicious has happened. I've been the one pushing for an autopsy and for there to be a review of any operational cameras around town. Based on what you told me at the scene, it seems unlikely that this guy drove the car to that spot." I already knew that the morgue people had said the time of death didn't meet up, that was what the woman from the railway investigation team had told me.

"You believe me?" I asked.

"Why wouldn't I?" he laughed. "You don't lie to the police anymore, do you?"

He was reminiscing. I felt as though my stomach was filled with swarms of butterflies as the incident he was referring to came rushing back. James and I had snuck out to meet up in the woods. We were both supposed to be locked away at home to prepare for some upcoming exam or doing homework or something. Either way we weren't supposed to be together.

That made us want to see each other all the more.

We met up and ran to the trees, not far from where Kari had the cookout actually, and there we had whiled away the hours doing the things that teenagers in love do. For some reason, James' parents had absolutely freaked out when they'd realized he wasn't in his room where he was supposed to be.

Black Bridge is a small, often quiet, town. This meant that when his mom had called the police to report him missing – keep in mind we'd probably only been gone an hour at that point – they responded by sending officers out to look for him. Why not? There wasn't anything else going on that day.

We'd heard them coming, two sets of booted feet marching through the trees towards us. When they spotted James I could see that they were about to launch into a rant about *something*, so I quickly announced that we were helping a friend look for her dog. I said that Spot – the name of the fake dog – had broken loose from his collar and run towards the stream so we were out looking for him.

This backfired in that the police decided to join *that* search and were out in the fields for hours with flashlights. I got into trouble for that, mostly with my mom. The Sergeant that was in charge of the Black Bridge police at that time had it out for my entire family. By all accounts my mother and her sisters had been rebellious, combative and disrespectful in their teen years, so had been labeled public nuisances.

On the assumption that the apple didn't fall far from the tree, that same Sergeant watched me like a hawk. When he had died, Digby got a promotion. He was blissfully unaware of the Sutton sisters and their reign of terror, so I was off the hook. James smirked at me and sat down on the sofa. I took a seat in the armchair that faced him and could feel my cheeks blushing at the memory he had just brought up.

"No, my lying days are behind me," I smirked. James reached into his top pocket and pulled out a small note pad, I could see from here that he had written down some questions.

"What do you know about the guy in the car?"

"It's Lionel Basset, from Diversity Capital. I don't know much else about him other than that, but you were at the town hall meeting too, right? You'd seen him before," I replied.

"You saw me there?" he grinned. "Where were you standing?"

"At the back with Kari and Will. I was covering the meeting for the paper and it got out of hand pretty fast once my mom started screaming at Stephen."

"She's never been boring, you have to hand it to her," he hummed, noting something down. "Okay, when you said you were covering it for the paper, did you record anything?"

I furrowed my brow at him, prompted him to elaborate.

"Like you said, it got out of hand fast. I know people were throwing stuff at Counselor Berry and the Diversity Capital guys, we began evacuating the hall and people were running in all directions. I didn't actually see *who* was doing the throwing."

"I took a video of it all," I said. "It's on my phone, I haven't actually watched it back yet. Do you think one of the people at the meeting might have killed that guy?"

"At this point I'm just trying to gather information," he replied. "Digby has no interest in dragging out an investigation, he likes dressing up as a police officer more than he likes *being* one."

"Ooh, sounds like there's a story there," I teased.

"You don't even want to know," he sighed. "I shouldn't be bad-mouthing the Sergeant to a civilian, either."

"Civilian?" I laughed.

"You know what I mean," he smiled. "Look, I think that *if* Lionel Basset was murdered, and for arguments sake let's go with that theory, then the motive is likely related to the fact that he had rolled into town to buy up the green belt, right?"

"Right."

"You saw how that town hall meeting went, people are livid about it. I think the fields are nice and all but I don't think they're worth killing over." I thought back to everything my grandmother had said about those fields, about what was buried out there.

"Mmhmm," I nodded. If there was a whole community of witches in this town, like my mom had said, then they might be angry enough to kill over it. But I had absolutely no idea what witches were capable of, or what their motivations were, or even *who* they were in this town. There was also no way I was mentioning any of this to James, he'd think I was insane.

"I have tried to contact Diversity Capital in the states but no one seems to want to speak to me. I don't know if they are still in town or where there were staying or anything," he shrugged. I remember the hotel key card that I'd found in the dirt by the fence last night.

"Probably the Belmont, right? It's the nicest hotel in town and they were all rich, it makes sense," I offered.

"You're probably right," he said. He folded the notepad closed and returned it to his top pocket. "I have to take off, but would I be able to come back later and you could show me the video of the meeting? I can bring Mexican food!"

"Is there a Mexican restaurant in Black Bridge that I don't know about?" I laughed.

"I was actually just offering to make us fajitas, I know they're your favorite. Or at least they were at some point."

"Still my favorite. If you ever offer me fajitas and I turn them down, that's how you'd know my body has been stuffed into a locker somewhere and you're talking to my android-replacement," I asserted, before I remembered. "But I *do* actually have plans for tonight, or rather my mom has plans for me."

"So you *have* been replaced by an android?" he teased. "How about tomorrow then? I can speak to a few people on my list between now and then anyway, it will probably help. I've shared my theories with Sergeant Digby but he couldn't care less."

"It's a date!" I smiled. "I mean, you know, it's a... like a friendly dinner with friends. Old friends. Friendly fajitas."

"I knew what you meant," he laughed. He checked the time on his watch and then look horror-struck. "Oh great, Vic is gonna kill me. Tomorrow, here, fajitas are on me!"

He stood up and ran for the door, a parting wave before he broke into a sprint up the street. He was heading somewhere to meet his girlfriend, of course he was.

"I don't know what's going on between you two, but I could cut the sexual tension in here with a knife," Pepper said, stretching his front legs dramatically.

"Please don't say the word 'sexual', you're a kitten and this whole thing is weird enough," I groaned.

"You're welcome for the transformation by the way, his eyes nearly blew out of their sockets!"

"He has a girlfriend, there's nothing going on," I replied.

"Sure, and I'm Marie Antoinette. His body might have run off to meet that other woman, but his mind will be right here with you all day, mark my words."

I didn't necessarily relish taking romantic advice from a cat, or any advice for that matter, but I couldn't help hoping that he was right.

11

"I just think it's a little much for the restaurant, that's all," my mom whined. I had bid farewell to Pepper to comply with my mom's request for assistance, and this was the thanks I got. Typical.

"I told you…" I whispered, not wanting to speak too loudly in case anyone else heard me, although we were here after hours and there were no customers. "I didn't do my makeup, the cat did."

"And why would your familiar be giving you a makeover?" she scowled.

"Can I just get these cookies made without being interrogated about my every move?"

"Fine. The order for tomorrow is up on the ticket and we also need two batches for tonight."

"Tonight?"

"Yes, the coven meeting. It's my turn to provide the snacks and as you were going to be making cookies anyway it seemed sensible to just make a triple batch of the white chocolate chunk ones so we could take some with us," Mom nodded.

"If *you* are responsible for the snacks, then shouldn't *you* be the one making them?" I countered.

"Don't be pedantic, Elizabeth."

I rolled my eyes and turned to spot my cousin Deanna walk through the door.

"She roped you into this too, huh?" I called out.

"You bet! Although I was told if I play my cards right that I can get a lunch made on the house this week," she replied.

"How come nobody offered *me* a free lunch?" I complained.

"You are being paid, Elizabeth," Mom shrugged.

"Wait, what?" Deanna gasped. "If you were paying me I could buy *three* lunches!"

"You are helping out family, what greater reward could there be?" mom smirked.

"Er, minimum wage?" Deanna muttered.

"I heard that! Besides, don't you both have more important things to talk about? Perhaps the fact that Elizabeth will be attending our coven meeting tonight?"

"Excuse me!" Deanna screeched, a pitch so high and scratchy that I thought the windows might shatter. "They finally told you?"

"How long have you known?" I asked.

"Liz, it's been, like, fourteen years," Deanna grimaced. "It was getting awkward to be honest with you. I got a hard time from people at school for having a girl in my family that wasn't using her powers."

"How was I supposed to know?"

"I don't know. My parents sat me down and had the talk and that was it."

I sighed and thought about the fact that everyone in my family seemed to know about this except me. Deanna wasn't just my cousin, but my friend, so the fact that she had participated in the big lie was all the more frustrating.

"Hey, I would have told you if I was allowed," Deanna offered.

"Don't be hard on her, Elizabeth. Just because my sister chose to let *her* children know early, doesn't mean that everybody was supposed to do it. I just thought I was protecting you and maybe that wasn't the smartest choice but I don't think now is the time to point fingers of blame in any direction," Mom smiled, flicking on the ovens to warm up and handing aprons to Deanna and me.

"What do you mean 'now is not the time', I have known about this since this morning. Now feels like a perfect time to me," I scowled.

"Oh don't be such a sour puss, just get those cookies made. I've sent a group text out to let everyone know that you're coming, so I wouldn't be surprised if you get some gifts tonight! People will be expecting thank you cards, I assume you still have that stationary set I bought for you last Christmas," Mom said, waiting for my response.

"Sure," I lied.

"Would either of you like the radio on while you work?"

"Why not?" I smiled. My mom switched it on, adjusted the volume to 'barely audible' levels, then grabbed her keys.

"I've just remembered I have to take care of a few things before the meeting, are you girls alright to finish up the baking and the food prep for the big order? There's a key by the coffee machine to lock up once you're done and Deanna can show you where to go once you're ready, okay bye!"

My mom left the building without pausing for breath long enough for us to respond. Neither of us were shocked by her lack of involvement in the food side of things tonight, but I *was* surprised that Deanna and I had once again been lured into the trap of helping out in the restaurant while my mom did nothing.

"The audacity of that woman is unparalleled," I remarked.

"Yeah, did she just refer to us both as 'girls' too? I am *this* close to having a mortgage, I'm a woman now!" Deanna announced.

"Jeez, is being a homeowner what it takes to be seen as an adult now? I'm screwed."

"Things aren't that bad," she assured me. "You had a little set back, but you're home with all of us now and this new phase of your life is going to be the best one!"

"Are you referring to the phase that involves me sleeping in my grandparent's old bedroom? Or the one where I'm being yelled at by my high school boyfriend's new girlfriend? Or *maybe* you mean the one where I'm working a part-time job for an ass-hat at the local paper?"

"The one that has you learning about your powers, dummy! I wouldn't worry so much about Victoria, anyway. I think you shoving her onto the floor last night is probably going to have her keeping a distance for a while."

"I didn't shove her," I said, weighing out a huge quantity of flour and wafting away the cloud that plumed as I poured it into a bowl on the scales.

"Did you do that with magic? That's pretty cool. I once had a guy yell at me in a parking lot and I used my magic to make his exhaust fall off, it's a satisfying feeling don't get me wrong, but you just need to be careful."

"What do you mean?" I asked.

"There's a bunch of rules about showing non-magical people what we've got going on, I'm sure you'll get some super boring leaflet about it at the coven meeting tonight but to give you the abridged version, regular people should never see you use your magic. The more experienced you get the better you will be at using it discreetly, but you're not there yet."

"Is Victoria Cressley a witch?"

"Nope!" Deanna smirked, tipping chocolate chunks into the dough that was now coming together after I'd stirred in butter and sugar. "She's as useful as a chocolate teapot and about as interesting as a monopoly rule book. James won't be with her much longer now that you're back."

"Why does everyone keep saying that?"

"Who else has said it?"

"Well there's you, Kari... er, probably more people behind my back but you two have said it straight to my face. For crying out loud, I had a cat show up today and *he* said it!"

"You have a familiar?" Deanna screeched, again in a tone so shrill my eardrums were quaking.

"Yeah, he's a fuzzy little kitten called Pepper and he's way more

CURIOSITY KILLED THE WITCH

annoying that I thought a cat could be. You know how cats are super irritating sometimes and completely self-obsessed, it turns out if you give them the ability to talk all of those personality traits are even worse."

"Familiars choose you, Lizzie. I've never had one and I've never been more jealous in my life. You've been a witch for like twenty seconds and you have one just rocking up to your front door!"

"I think my grandmother brought him actually, the pair of them were in my living room when I woke up this morning."

"That makes sense then," Deanna said. "Your family is a pretty big deal, I bet that cat couldn't believe his luck when he realized there was a Sutton witch in need of a familiar."

"You're a Sutton witch too!"

"Yeah, but you're the first daughter of a first daughter. It's like, a *thing* so you're slightly more important than the rest of the cousins. Although if you say that out loud then you might get slapped," she teased. "Rumor has it that Marla's baby is gonna be a boy, and it's caused *quite* the scandal."

"What's scandalous about that?" I asked, thinking of my pregnant cousin and how she had recently cancelled her baby shower. I had figured it was because baby showers can be long and boring, but maybe there was more to it.

"The power in the Sutton family is passed through the women. If Marla is having a boy then it's like, *urgh*, you know?"

"Not really, but then again nothing makes sense anymore." I used an ice-cream scoop to portion out the cookie dough onto the baking sheets, spacing them out perfectly to avoid them merging into one giant blob in the oven. "James came to the house today," I confessed, blurting it out as the words needed to escape, as if I were expelling a poison.

Deanna slammed her scoop down on the steel counter and put her hands on her hips. "I have been here almost forty minutes and *this* is the first I'm hearing about it?"

"I knew you'd make it into a big thing, which maybe it is, but I'm just feeling like a lot is going on right now and you are a great person to bounce ideas off," I shrugged.

"What's your idea? That you and James Webster should go French in the woods like you did in the good old days?" she cackled as she opened the oven door for me to slide the trays in. I blushed.

"No. He is with someone and I should move on, I mean, I broke his heart and he shouldn't even want to be anywhere near me."

"Do you think less of him for still having his eye on you? Because you're aging like a fine wine, my friend. You must have been turning heads left, right and center in London. They don't make people like you in the city, that's just a fact!"

"I dated a little in London, you know, the odd coffee shop lunch or a silent couple of hours in a movie theatre. I don't want to just fall into old habits because I'm home, I don't want anything to happen with James because it's just *comfortable.* Real love isn't just comfortable, it's supposed to be fiery and exciting, can't stop thinking about each other stuff."

"Where are you getting that from? Some Nicholas Sparks book?" Deanna said. "If anything happens between you and James again I can promise you it's not because you're an old habit. When you left he was a mess, but I feel like he has his spark back since you came home. I know you were avoiding him, but I think him just knowing that you were nearby was enough."

I felt guilty that my avoidance had been so obvious. Did James know about it? Since seeing him at the town hall I had to admit that he had been on my mind, even more so since our argument on the train tracks. We *were* fiery and exciting.

We sat on a pair of stools and watched the cookie dough change shape and begin to turn a golden color around the edges. Once the timer rang out, Deanna pulled the trays out of the oven and set them on the side to cool.

"Are you nervous about the coven meeting?" she asked.

"Totally! Is there going to be a test? I literally only found out about all this a few hours ago."

"Ha, no test required. Your grandmother runs the thing so I'm sure everyone will go easy on you."

I gave her a curious look. "Since when did she run a cov— you know what, I'm not even going to ask. Let's just box up what we are supposed to take with us and let's get out of here. If we wait much longer then my mother will return and give us another list of jobs to do."

"Oh she won't have a problem giving that to us tonight," Deanna laughed.

The town hall had a basement, this was news to me. Deanna and I arrived at the building and she grabbed the door handle tightly, twisted and pulled, revealing a set of stairs twisting downwards. I had been through this door dozens of times in my life, and I had never seen this before.

"On nights when the coven is meeting we can access the stairs," Deanna offered by way of an explanation. "Only witches can get down here, we won't be disturbed." Oh, I was disturbed alright.

I don't know what I had been expecting, but a slightly larger turnout was probably it. Seven women, four of which had thick silver curls crowning their heads, all turned to look my way as I entered. There was also my mother, my grandma and my friend Kari. I caught the expression on my friend's face, one of quiet panic.

"I would have told you," she began, her hands waving about energetically as she launched into her speech, one that I imagined she had been practicing all day. "I wanted to, obviously, but it wasn't right for *me* to go over anyone's head and this is more of a family thing, you know? Like, I found out from my mom and she found out from hers, it's a tradition! I'm a descendant of the Salem witches, Liz, it's a pretty big deal! You know how many times I wanted to brag about that but couldn't?"

"Oh Kari dear, do sit down," my mother sighed. "This is not the time to start ranting about Salem."

"Although we owe a lot to our ancestors," my grandma added.

"Yes, of course, we're very grateful," mom muttered without a hint of sincerity. I imagined her to always be the biggest force in any room, but not tonight. This was a side of my grandma that I hadn't seen before and the dynamic in my family was very different in this basement. My mom wasn't in charge, I couldn't help but feel a smirk spread across my face.

"It was a last minute meeting, Lizzie, otherwise we would have had the whole coven show up. I think there is a Love Island finale on tonight or something," my grandmother shrugged. "Anyway, let's get started with our business, shall we?"

This prompted the group to take their seats in a circle, as if we were all attendants at a group therapy session. The basement seemed to have windows that were letting in shafts of light from the street lamps, but we had gone down a flight of stairs to get in here. Nothing about this place made much sense.

"Lizzie, care to introduce yourself?" grandma prompted. I swallowed hard, looked to my cousin on the left of me, then Kari on my right.

"Stand up," Kari whispered, nudging me with her arm. I got to my feet.

"Hi, hello, how's it going?" I said, a polite smile plastered on my face as I looked around the room. The cliched advise about public speaking suddenly flashed into my mind, *'Imagine them all in their underwear and you won't feel nervous'*. Did that ever really work? Why would that help calm me down?

I looked at the group, unsure of what to say. *Underwear.* "My name is Elizabeth, but you can call me Liz, or Lizzie, Beth if you like. I don't care for Bess, so maybe don't say that." What was I even talking about? I had just been listing my own nicknames for what felt like forever and I had no idea what the format of this introduction was supposed to be. I looked at the woman directly across from me and realized that she was now in a progressed state of undress.

There was a retired stranger sitting in this basement in her underwear. Matching emerald green silks, if you must know.

"Oh, Liz," my grandmother sighed. "Did you think picturing us all in our underwear would help? You can't really do that sort of thing now that you have access to your powers. Are you okay, Jean?"

"Of course! I don't often get a chance to show off my lingerie, so I relish the opportunity," she giggled, snapping her fingers to make her clothes reappear.

I began to wish the ground would swallow me whole so that I didn't have to face the embarrassing nightmare that I'd just created, but then I got scared that I might actually summon a black hole in the floor so quickly thought of something else.

"Jean, I am so sorry," I blushed. You could fry an egg on my cheeks.

"It's not the first time it's happened, don't worry," she smiled. I prayed no one asked her a follow up question about that.

"Maybe it's best that you just sit down, sweetheart," grandma suggested. I didn't need telling twice. "This is my granddaughter, she's new to this as you can see." The heat of my cheeks increased another few degrees. "As always, it takes a village to raise a witch so I trust you will treat her well, be patient, and encourage her when needed. She has also brought cookies…"

This caused a buzz among the older ladies and they quickly took to their feet to hunt out the baked goods. Did that mean the meeting was over? That was less than five minutes, beginning to end. Was this normal?

"Is that it?" I asked.

"You were late, Elizabeth. We started it without you," Mom huffed.

"Wh— I was at the restaurant baking, you said that—"

"It doesn't matter now, no use trying to wriggle out of trouble," she said. Sometimes I wish I had the nerve to just have an emotional outburst, but I knew it would cause more problems than it solved. "We discussed the situation with the green belt, word on the street is that they are hoping to 'break ground' on the building project as soon as possible. We have to stop it, *you* have to stop it."

"What? Why me?"

"You're a journalist, aren't you? Why don't you put all that 'skill' to good use and dig up some dirt on Diversity Capital that can sink this thing and save our town!"

I didn't appreciate the air quotes around the word 'skill', but the idea that my mother had even the slightest confidence in my abilities was monumental. If it weren't for the sour look on her face, this would almost be a touching moment between us.

"I'll see what I can find," I nodded. Where would I even start?

12

Thankfully, sleep had come quickly. My grandma and I had walked home together, given that she was staying in the house with me until she disappeared back to her Greek cruise with my grandfather. She had assured me that zapping the clothes off an old lady wasn't all that bad, and that she had done far worse when she was starting out with magic.

So far I'd managed to stop a train, push over a thin woman and humiliate a boomer. Actually, Jean wasn't humiliated, she was very proud of her body it seemed. If it hadn't been for Pepper showing me how to use my magic in the garden yesterday then I'd be about ready to change my name and move to a town where no one knew me.

A knock on the door caused me to sit bolt up-right, like Dracula in his coffin. Pepper was curled up on the pillow beside my face, the pads of his fuzzy feet pressed against my forehead, meaning that when I'd lurched into a seated position I'd narrowly avoided having my eyes scratched out.

"Who knocks at this time?" he groaned. I looked over at the clock.

"It's after nine, it's socially acceptable to start invading people's privacy now," I complained, swinging my feet onto the floor and standing up to peer out of the window that looked over the street. I could just about see the top of a police officer's hat. *James.* "Do that thing again, the magic make-me-hot spell."

"What are you talking about?" Pepper stretched his paws and sat up to squint at me as the sunlight burst through the gap in the curtains behind me.

"Yesterday you did a thing, a makeover thing, do it again. I am begging you."

"Oh, is lover boy back?" the cat smirked.

"It's not like that, I just—"

"You just want to look hot for your 'friend'. You want a figure-hugging dress that accentuates your figure and a full face of make up to signify just how platonic your relationship is," he laughed. "Who are you trying to fool?"

"Maybe it's complicated, maybe it's not. I just don't want to answer the front door looking like a swamp monster because—"

"Oh James, dear, come on in. Lizzie won't be a minute, you're here for her I take it?" my grandmother cooed. Great, she'd answered the door.

"Thank you," he replied.

"Tea or coffee? What's your poison?" she asked. The two of them were downstairs chatting away like old friends and Pepper was watching me closely, amusement evident in his expression.

"Oh boy, you really want to impress this guy. There's a story there, and I want every detail!" he mewed.

"Now? We don't have time for me to outline our entire relationship!"

"Give me the short version," he smiled. He really wasn't backing down.

"Dated as teens, madly in love, job came up in London, he didn't want to go but I did, we broke up," I blurted.

"And you were both still 'madly in love' when you left I take it? Hmm, interesting," he said, pacing up and down the bed.

"I made a choice, and in hindsight it was the wrong one," I shrugged, almost defeatedly as I admitted out loud to a *cat* that my life wasn't going how I'd planned it.

"You get one more, on the house," he said. He stopped still and turned to face me, wiggled his nose and my baggy pajamas changed into a pair of smart jeans, a button-up white shirt and a heavy gold chain around my neck. I looked like a ran a big company, it was the most professional I'd ever looked.

"Why this?" I asked.

"He is downstairs talking about you both going to some hotel to ask questions about Diversity Capital. I don't know much about that, but it sounds serious, so I thought you should be dressed like you had a proper job."

"Gee, thanks," I sighed. My hair was pulled up into a ponytail, a quick glance into a mirror let me know that this was probably what I *should* have worn when I worked for the paper in London. Instead I had worn old band t-shirts and black skinny jeans, I owned one really smart dress and it had been something my mom had bought for me to attend a family wedding years ago. I should probably update my wardrobe to reflect my age, but I didn't have that kind of disposable income yet.

"Like I said, this is the last one on the house," he reminded me.

"What does that mean?" I asked, worried that I'd entered into some unholy arrangement with a magical creature that would lead to sinister things.

"I'm your familiar, not your butler. I enhance your magic, help you learn, generally improve your life with my delightful presence. You need to figure out how to do some of these things for yourself," he said.

"Okay, well thank you for helping me today. I appreciate it," I smiled. I left the room and bounced down the first few steps with a giddy gait that betrayed my excitement to see James. I paused, took a deep breath, then walked down the remainder of the staircase calmly.

"Oh Lizzie, look who's here," grandma grinned, winking at me and pointing at the police officer sitting in her best armchair with a cup of tea in his hands. I doubted if there was a single man in all of England that looked better in a police uniform that James Webster. *He has a girlfriend*. That woman is mad as a box of frogs, but it's none of my business.

"Good morning," he smiled, his eyes sparkling under the living room lights.

"Hi."

The look of sheer joy on my grandmother's face was distracting me from enjoying the moment. I could see she was in one of her puckish moods. "Would you like a hot drink? Or maybe a cold shower?" she teased.

"Coffee would be great," I replied. "No milk no sugar."

"You still drink your coffee black? I thought you'd have come back from London with a taste for more complicated drinks, I thought you'd be all 'americano' this and 'latte' that," James laughed.

"Do you think those are complicated? You live a very sheltered life," I said, sitting down on the sofa and waiting for him to bring up the reason for the visit.

"Fajitas," he blurted out. "I said I'd make you fajitas tonight and I would still like to, I just figured that if we wanted to speak to the people at the hotel then we should head over sooner rather than later. If you're busy this morning then I can go by myself. Dressed up like that... you look like you have somewhere special to be."

Be still my beating heart. There was still the nervous energy that had used to consume our every interaction when we had first started dating all those years ago. Every move overanalyzed, every thought a thought of him. So much time had passed and yet he could still make my skin tingle all over with just a turn of phrase.

He was staring at me. I gulped.

"I don't have anywhere to be. What could be more important than trying to catch a killer, anyway?" I grinned.

"Here's your coffee," grandma announced, turning the mug handle toward me so I could take it from her. "So are you two planning to sneak around town together hunting down bad guys like a couple of beagles on a fox hunt?"

"I got lost somewhere in that analogy, but yes," James nodded.

"We're not sneaking, just working together," I clarified.

"Oh, sure," she winked. I saw James grin out the corner of my eye and I tried desperately to keep a neutral expression. "Victoria knows who you are planning to spend your day with, does she?"

Why would she ask that?

"She knows I'm working today," he said, expertly dodging the question.

"We should get going, we don't want to be late," I announced, rising to my feet.

"Late? For the hotel that has someone on the reception desk twenty-four hours a day?" Grandma laughed. "Oh yeah, better hurry along to meet with the person that has no idea you're coming and isn't waiting for you! Good luck!" At that she walked out of the living room into the kitchen, her laughter bouncing off the walls as she went.

"This is why I need my own place," I muttered as I walked to the front door. Pepper bounded down the stairs and began rubbing his body against my ankles.

"Who's this little guy then? I remember seeing him yesterday," James said, crouching down to fuss him behind the ear.

"Pepper," I answered.

"I never had you down as a cat person, you were always so into the idea of getting a dog."

Pepper gave me a look that let me know that we would be discussing that later.

"Cats are great," I replied. "I like cats just as much as dogs!"

"I thought you said that cats were totally pointless as pets because they just move into your neighbor's houses the first chance they get so they can eat six dinners, you said—"

"Wow, you have a great memory for everything I've ever said about cats," I interrupted. "Maybe we can talk about the dead guy on the train tracks instead!"

Pepper was never going to let me forget any of that, I already knew it. We made our way out onto the street and began heading in the direction of The Belmont. It was one of those English hotels that looked as though it once held regal ballroom dances, dinners for the upper echelons of society and perhaps housed a Duke or Duchess.

Its exterior had been designed to maximize the light that could filter in to the dining room on the ground floor. Bay windows jutting out into the lawn that wrapped around the front of the building so that couples could eat with a view of the sky. Now they would get a view of the row of houses across the street that obstructed the line of sight to the rolling hills beyond.

A large wooden sign with 'The Belmont' painted in cursive had been staked into the ground to advertise its presence, as if the huge letters above the front door didn't already do that.

James and I hadn't spoken all that much on the journey across town. We had wormed through the streets of Black Bridge in relative silence for the first few minutes, before I finally remembered to mention that I'd found a key card for The Belmont on the ground by the field where we'd had the cookout.

"You think it was Lionel's?" he asked.

"I have no way to know that until we hand it in at the reception desk, I just thought it was odd that's all. It was what made me realize that the guys from Diversity Capital were probably staying there. I haven't thought about the Belmont in years, I almost forgot it was here," I shrugged. It was coming into view now, in all its sun-faded glory.

"I think most people have, that's the problem. Their nightly rates are so high that they are never over twenty percent capacity, I'm surprised they are still open."

I remembered the prices. We had once looked at pooling our money together and spending the night in one of the rooms, just the two of us with a king-sized bed and room service. Obviously two teenagers couldn't afford that, I would have had to work thirty hours a day for two weeks at the restaurant to earn that kind of money. It wasn't feasible.

"How do you want to do this?" I asked. "Do I say that I'm a journalist?"

"Well you are, aren't you?" he smirked. "Let me do the talking initially, see how cooperative the staff are before we start dropping the 'J' bomb."

"Why do you think me being a journalist holds more weight than you being with the police?" I laughed.

"People get edgy around the police, clam up, keep their secrets. I think journalism gives you a foot in the door because when *you* say you are out to gather information no one feels as threatened. Or at least that's what I learned in a true-crime documentary once. Would you agree?"

He wasn't wrong. I'd been at crime scenes where witnesses were hesitant to speak to the cops, but would gladly offer me quotes that I could print. They trusted me when I said that they could remain anonymous.

"Good morning, welcome to The Belmont. Do you have a booking?" A man in his late forties was wearing a red velvet waistcoat over a white shirt, a bow tie sat off-balance around his neck. He was dressed like one of those wind-up monkeys that banged cymbals together.

"No, we were hoping to ask you a few questions about a guest you may have had staying here recently," James said. "I'm Officer Webster, and—"

"I know who you are," the man scowled. "You arrested my father in his retirement home."

"You did *what?*" I gasped, completely unable to keep my reaction in.

"Well I think… the thing with that is…" James was flustered. This was not the beginning to this interaction that any of us had been hoping for.

"Was he right to do so?" I asked.

"My dad was selling some of his prescription meds to his friends in the home, so I suppose *technically* he wasn't doing the right thing but—" the man said, his face screwed up as he tried to wrestle with the question I'd asked.

"It's illegal to sell prescription-only medication like that," James countered.

"What was he selling?" I asked.

"Enbrel and Caverject," the man replied. "One is for arthritis and the other one… well when a man get's older sometimes he can't—"

"Please don't say another word," I squeaked, cutting him off. I didn't need to know about an old man selling his 'performance enhancing' drugs to his friends.

"He didn't get jail time," James said. "There was a fine and I think he was given community service hours. He got off lightly!"

"Hmm," the man huffed.

"Okay… well now that we've dealt with that, could we ask you about Lionel Bassett?" I asked.

"It is not hotel policy to give out information about guests to strangers," he grunted. "And after all, we have to be careful around this one," he jabbed a finger in James' direction, "because he will arrest you for absolutely anything. If I violate our company terms then he'll probably drag me out of here in handcuffs!"

"Your dad was selling pills for erec—"

"Hey!" I yelled, stopping James from bringing it up again. No pun intended. "Look, did you hear about the incident on the train tracks?" A blank stare followed. "The car? The dead man *inside* the car?" Still nothing. "Have you been out of town or something? One of the guys trying to buy the green belt was found dead and I think he was staying here, could you tell me if I'm right?"

"Why do you think he was staying here?" the man asked, folding his arms and raising an eyebrow. He looked like a seven-year-old that was convinced they were winning a debate, all sass.

"I have this key card, for one thing," I said, pulling it out of my pocket and waving it around.

"Why do *you* have that?"

"I found it, can you tell me which room it belongs to? And who you have checked in to that room?" I smiled sweetly in the way that I used to as a child when I asked for more dessert, hey if he was bringing childish tactics into play then so would I.

"I suppose I could do that," he agreed. I wasn't actually expecting that to work, and gave James a side eye to suggest as much. He raised his eyebrows and nodded gently, a sign that he was impressed. The receptionist inserted the key card into a small machine that was wired up to the computer, a beeping sound alerted us that the scan was complete.

"Well?" I pressed.

"This is for room ten, Lionel Bassett," he replied. "Diversity Capital booked four rooms for the week, the rest of them are still here I think. They had room nine, ten, eleven and twelve."

"Is there any chance we could look in Lionel's room?" James asked.

"Why would I allow that to happen?" the man scoffed.

"We are currently operating on the theory that Lionel was in fact murdered, that his placement in the car *on* the train tracks was actually an attempt to cover up the murder, the assailant likely planned that the train collision would be so enormous that it would obscure the actual cause of death. If our theory is correct, then there could be evidence in Lionel's room to help us identify his killer but your decision here might be classed as obstruction of justice which would *almost* make you an accomplice to the crime."

The silence that followed was like a held breath. The only sound was the blood in my ears, gently reminding me that my heart was now racing. Was anything I'd just said accurate? I had no idea. But I really wanted to get into that room and sometimes a confident monologue is the only way to get things done, or at least that's what action films have always told me.

"Are you a police officer?" the man asked, now visibly shaken.

"I'm a journalist, my name's Elizabeth Sutton. I'm with The Herald," I announced. *With* The Herald. That had a nice ring to it. Maybe a confident monologue in David Dawson's direction would convince him to take me on full time.

"Sutton? I know that name. Your family owns that restaurant, the one with the good omelets," he muttered.

"They specialize in sandwiches really, my dad takes care of the eggs but I don't—"

"Yes, her family owns the restaurant," James cut in, nudging me with an elbow.

"Okay, well as you're a journalist then I'll let you in. Just make sure my name stays out of it, anything you find you just say you found it in the park or something," he said, leaning in conspiratorially as he pulled the key card out of the machine and walked round to the front of the desk. I didn't feel the need to point out that I wasn't currently working on an article, all I'd said was that I was *with* The Herald, which was also not exactly true.

"Sure," I grinned, my eyes betrayed the surprise I felt that this had actually worked. We were guided up two flights of stairs and straight to a dark, wooden door with a golden plaque in the center: Room 10.

"Take as much time as you need, the room's paid up for another day or two," the receptionist said as he handed me the key. "Just make sure that you keep my name out of it and don't say you found anything *in* the hotel because I could lose my job!" He shut the door and I realized that keeping his name out of it would be easy given that he never told us what it was. James and I turned to each other, then to the desk covered in stacks of papers.

Hopefully there was something useful in here. "Take this," I said, handing James a level-arch file that felt as though it weighed forty pounds. The page on the top of the closest pile of papers was littered with legal jargon and contract-type language. This was going to take hours to decipher.

After forty-five minutes of mindless reading, I found something.

13

"*Here*," I said, taking the page over to the bed where James had reclined to read through the file. "This page has the signatures of a bunch of councilors that agreed to sell off the land. Natasha said that she was approached to make a website for the new retail place that was going to be built, she said it was already a done deal."

"I remember. It was all of her team, all of the guys from Diversity Capital and Stephen Berry at that meeting," he added. "It is probably time to speak with Stephen."

"You think he's going to admit that he already sold off the green belt? If people find out he's going to get eggs thrown at his house for the next six months!"

"Yeah I know, which gives him a reason to want this kept quiet, right? He might be more cooperative with us once we tell him what we know. Did you say the video from the town hall meeting is on your phone?" he asked.

"Yeah."

"If we watch it now we can try to identify the people that were throwing stuff, the ones yelling the loudest, maybe present the short list to Stephen and ask if he's had any other confrontations with those people."

"The loudest person at the meeting was my mother, I don't need to check the video for that," I smirked. He was sat with his back against the headboard, the pillows arranged for maximum comfort. I got myself into a similar position beside him, loaded up the video and pressed play.

As Lionel began speaking I noticed Stephen in the background opening a small chocolate bar and taking a bite. This was shortly before the yelling started. He had barely had chance to chew before he was trying to defend himself against the barrage of accusations being thrown his way, then the first shoe was thrown through the air.

"Okay, so it looks as though the old folks on the front row were yelling, then the shoe came from back there," James said, leaning across me slightly to point at my screen. I could smell the scent of his cologne, mixed in with whatever shampoo he'd used when he showered this morning. "That looks like Ernie."

I felt my heart sink. If someone had killed Lionel, which we were quite sure was how this had all gone down, then *obviously* it was someone from around here because unless he'd been murdered by his banker buddies there was no one else around for miles. It was a small town, so it almost guaranteed that we would know whoever the murderer was, I just really wished for it to be a stranger, someone I didn't recognize.

"Yeah, it is," I agreed. I had paused the video and zoomed in on his face, his mouth contorted into a mid-shout fury that made his feelings clear. He ran a small store in a Lake District town, a national chain of grocery stores had already infiltrated Black Bridge, but if the green belt was sold off and a huge retail park was built then he might lose all of his business.

"We should speak to Ernie," James said, his voice heavy with the unspoken idea that we both shared. What if Ernie had killed Lionel? I already knew that the store wasn't open early on a Sunday morning, that's why I'd needed to cross the tracks to get the muscle-heat cream from somewhere else. What if he didn't have another alibi?

I grabbed the set of papers that pertained to the land purchase, making sure that I had hold of the signature page, and we left the room. My legs felt leaden as we walked back down the stairs, apprehensive about the conversation we were about to have with the shopkeeper I'd known most of my life.

"You found that on the grass outside, remember?!" the receptionist yelled when he saw what I was carrying.

"Sure," I replied.

When we stepped out into the sunlight, I found myself squinting, the brightness of the sky almost too much to bare.

"Do you really think Ernie could have done this?" I asked.

"No, but when people are about to lose something important they are capable of crazy things," James replied. His response felt loaded, but before I could think about it too much, a loud voice was bouncing off the walls of nearby houses. Victoria was marching up the street towards us, her hands balled into fists, and she had dark eyes like a shark with a scent of blood in the water.

"I knew you would do this, I knew it!" she shrieked.

"Vic, lower your voice," James said, raising his palms as if trying to calm a horse.

"No, you *promised* me that you didn't have feelings for her anymore and now you're in a hotel room together," she yelled. *Ah*. She doesn't know that we were just sat in there reading in silence, and I can see how this looks. People generally don't go into a hotel room alone for an hour just to read.

"Vic, we're working on a case—" James began.

"She's not a police officer, your lie doesn't even work!"

"She's helping with the investigation, you have to believe me," he pleaded. I was third wheel in an argument, and I was at feeling beyond awkward as I stood with my arms wrapped around stack of papers, trying to disappear into the background as this fight played out. Never mind. Victoria turned to me and I knew I was about to be on the receiving end of her accusations.

"Does it make you feel good to sleep with someone else's boyfriend?"

"We were reading papers, I know how it looks but—" I didn't even know why I was trying to reason with an unreasonable person.

"Why should I believe you? You're a snake in the grass, a real piece of work. I don't know what you see in her, James, I really don't. She broke your heart, she ruined your life, why are you even giving her the time of day? I wish I'd never found that stupid train ticket," she huffed, stomping her foot and turning to march away. What train ticket?

"Vic!" James called after her. She continued to storm away and he motioned to follow before turning back to me. "I'll speak to Ernie myself, don't worry about it. Maybe just head home and I'll see you later."

Before I had chance to say anything he was running down the street chasing a slim blonde with a temper. Maybe I could march myself into David's office at The Herald and propose my article into Lionel's death, or just outright demand that he hires me full time so I don't have to step foot behind the restaurant counter again. I hadn't brought a bag with me, so the first stop would be to take the papers home and *then* I could make my demands to the boss.

I hurried back through the streets of town, avoiding the road that would take me passed Ernie's place so that I didn't have to think about the guilt I felt for thinking he was capable of something terrible. I opened the front door of the house and walked in to find my grandmother in the living room. She was flanked by the older women that had been at the coven meeting the night before. Once again I'd let the witch situation slip my mind.

"There you are Lizzie, your cat has been asking after you," she smiled.

"Don't make me sound desperate," Pepper grumbled.

"I was just dropping off some stuff, but you can come with me this afternoon if you like?" I offered. "I can tuck you into a satchel or something."

Pepper contemplated it as I allowed the smell of freshly baked fruit cake corrupt my thoughts. On the coffee table there was a lemon drizzle loaf, fruit cake, half a dozen scones, and a plate of shortbread biscuits.

"What are you guys up to?" I asked.

"It's a coffee morning," Jean replied, standing to face me. "I'm wearing a lingerie set in sapphire blue today, in case you accidently blast my clothes off again."

"You did *what?!*" Pepper cackled. "I knew I should have gone to that coven meeting, you should have woken me so I could come along!"

"It was an accident, we don't all need to keep talking about it," I mumbled. "And since when did you do coffee mornings?" I asked my grandmother.

"It's for charity, Liz. We are raising money for cancer awareness," she nodded. "Since this little soiree began we've all learned that cancer is just, well it's bloody awful, isn't it, Jean?"

"Dreadful," Jean replied through a mouthful of scone crumbs.

"How much money have you raised between the five of you?"

"Five pounds sixty pence," grandma announced. "I don't carry cash if I can help it, I think we found three of those pound coins between the sofa cushions."

"I will make a donation online, providing I can figure out how to do it," another woman declared.

"Rebecca, you're one of the most tech savvy women I know, you can do it!" my grandmother cheered. Rebecca promptly adjusted her glasses and pulled out an old blackberry from her purse to wave at me as if to prove the statement true. The buttons on the phone were so worn that every letter had been rubbed off by typing fingers.

"Could I grab something to eat?" I asked, another waft of cake fragrance pulled me over like a siren song.

"You have to make a donation," grandma replied. I was quite sure that the three-pound coins that they'd found between the sofa cushions had been mine, but now wasn't the time to be tight with the purse strings. It was for 'charity' after all. I stuck a hand into the pocket of a coat hanging on the hooks by the front door and found a five-pound note, debated whether that was an extortionate price for one slice of cake or not, then handed over the money anyway.

The ladies chatted away about single, silver-foxes in town and ranked them in order of hottest to not-test, then by how rich they seemed. Occasionally the women would remember I was there, turn to Rebecca and nudge her to read another statistic from the 'Cancer Research UK' website.

"Oh, I just can't stop thinking about how there are approximately one thousand new cases diagnosed every day in this country. That's about one person every two minutes," she sighed. They all nodded along solemnly. *Smooth.*

"If we were to rank by best arse…" my grandmother continued.

"That's my cue to leave, Pepper are you coming?" I asked.

"Oh, and miss them talk about which wrinkly old butt they'd most like to squeeze?" he replied sarcastically.

"Get in the bag," I laughed, swinging the satchel over my shoulder and holding it open for him to jump inside.

"You'll have the house to yourself tonight, Liz," grandma shouted as I was halfway out the door. "Jean's hosting a game night at her house and we're all sleeping over."

"You have a better social life than I do and you've been back in town for two days! I thought you were supposed to be heading back to Greece to that cruise ship you've left grandad on."

"Oh, he's having a grand time without me. We decided it's probably best if we just stay in Black Bridge for the rest of the year and put the world travel on hold."

"Oh?" I asked.

"Don't worry, you can keep this house, I own another place on the other side of the tracks," she grinned.

"Since when do you have two houses? It's people like you that are preventing first-time buyers from getting on the property market," I complained.

"Oh don't get your knickers in a twist, I was telling you all that in case you want to have a little sleepover of your own tonight with a certain Officer Webster," she winked. I threw up in my mouth a little at the thought of my grandmother trying to orchestrate my sex life.

"*That* man has the best arse in Black Bridge, not a doubt in my mind," Jean offered as she took another bite of scone.

"I'm out of here!" I closed the door behind me and shuddered, as if trying to shake the memories of that conversation out of my head.

"I think those women are cougars," Pepper muttered from the satchel.

"My grandparents are still married!"

"Maybe they're swingers?"

"Do you want me to leave you in there with them, because I will happily step back inside to drop you off," I snapped.

"I'm good," he purred. "Where are we going anyway?"

"Two places, The Herald office, and then wherever Stephen Berry is likely to be," I replied.

When I didn't spot the Mercedes parked on the curb, that should have been my first clue. I went inside the offices anyway and looked around for any sign that David had been in the building recently.

"David?" I called out.

"Oh, you're funny," Gareth chuckled. He was one of the few people that had a full-time position with the paper, I think he handled all of the advertising and made sure that every single page featured some paid content. I think he also had to choose the positions of the ads to make sure that we didn't have a repeat of the lottery incident.

During one week of annual leave, Gareth had left his work in David's hands. This led to an article about three people being killed in a house fire on the other side of Lake Windemere being printed above an ad for the lottery which simply stated, '*You could be next!*'. A little dark for the paper that most people read over their morning coffee.

"What's funny?" I asked.

"David sent an email saying that he was working from home today, but I set up a fake Instagram account so I could follow him without him *knowing* I'm following him," Gareth explained. He swiveled in his office chair to face me. "He has been posting selfies this morning and tagged the pictures at the Statue of Franz Kafka."

"I don't know what that means."

"It's a tourist attraction in Prague, he's still away but hasn't filled out a form to request the extra days off so he's pretending he is at home. You'd actually be alarmed at how often he does that," Gareth sighed.

"Do you know when he'll be back?"

"Nope!" He spun the chair back to face his computer. "There is a two-day music festival starting there tomorrow, and I doubt he will be flying home before that."

"You've really done your homework," I remarked.

"My job doesn't take forty hours a week, so I play on Minecraft the rest of the time. Keeping track of the boss means I never get caught," he said, tapping a finger to his temple knowingly. "You've got to work smart, not hard."

"Noted."

With another failed excursion on the books, I decided to pay a visit to Councilor Stephen Berry. Beside the town hall was a small building which housed the offices of our local government. By local I mean *very* local, the only people ever really in there were teenagers looking for work experience, Stephen's assistant and a woman, Ellen, that dealt with the electoral role for the town. Given how many elections we had around here, it seemed weird that *her* job was one that required a staffed office at all times.

I stepped through the stone archway that towered over the thick wooden doors of the entrance and looked around at the bleak waiting room. Why you would be in here waiting for anything was anyone's guess. There was never a queue, so if you needed to speak to somebody then you were seen immediately.

"Yes?" election Ellen barked from her desk.

"I'm here to see Councilor Berry, is he here?" I asked. It was polite enough, but she still scowled at me as if I hadn't given the right honorable douchebag Berry enough respect in my sentence.

"She stood up and peered over a bookshelf that was half-blocking a window into a neighboring room. "It must be your lucky day," she sneered. "Down that hall, first door on the left. Knock first."

Maybe election Ellen was given a full-time job in an office by herself to keep her away from the other resident of Black Bridge.

Someone must have identified that she was a black hole that sucked the joy out anyone she spoke to, so did a public service by keeping her foul mood contained in this museum of staples and beige walls.

I dutifully knocked on the door when I made my way down the hallway, waited patiently for someone to open the door and welcome me inside. Instead I heard a lousy "yeah?" shouted in my direction. "Come in, I'm not getting up."

"This guy should be tied to a rocket headed for the sun," Pepper muttered from inside my satchel.

"Shh," I said, turning the handle and stepping inside. Stephen was sat with a calculator in one hand and a pen in the other. "Good afternoon," I offered, expecting the greeting to be returned.

"I'm counting carbs," he replied.

"Oh?" I said, feigning interest. Why would he tell me that? Who cares? No one *ever* wants to hear about your diet.

"What can I do for you?" he said, putting the calculator down and looking at me warily. His suit was ill-fitting, something I could see even though he was sat down. It was like a boy pretending to be a man by dressing up in daddy's suit.

"I know that you've signed off on the green belt sale," I announced. Maybe I should have played it a little cooler, not shown all my cards at once, but it was too late to do anything about it now.

"That's ridiculous," he scoffed.

"Is it? I know that you and the Diversity Capital people are looking to have a website made already, advertising your retail park. How much are they paying you for this, Steve?"

"It's Councilor Berry to you," he sneered. I suddenly had a great deal of confidence, likely because I had been tasked with saving the town by a coven of witches and I had to start as I meant to go on. I wanted a full-time job as a journalist with The Herald, I wanted Jean to stop trying to show me her underwear, and I wanted this piece of garbage to stop screwing over the people of this town.

"Oh really, *Steve?* Because I think when word of your arrangement gets out you won't be the councilor for much longer. I think we could have a snap election called by the end of the week, don't you? I"

"Listen, Bess," he said, leaning back in his chair as he dared to use a nickname for me that I didn't approve of, "this move was inevitable. This town is like a wrinkled old lady that no one wants to look at anymore, way past its prime. I want to give this town a little face lift, turn her into a hotter model."

"There was so much wrong with what you just said I don't even know where to begin," I said, my eyes rolled back in my head with disdain.

"The people of this cesspit town don't know what's good for them, but *I* do. You see, once they have a cinema on their doorstep and a few thousand more residents to sell their wares too they'll be beating down my door to give me thank you cards. I just need a bit more time to convince them that it's the right thing, then we can move right ahead with it."

"But you've already signed the papers," I countered.

"Can you prove it?" he smirked.

"Yeah, I can actually. I've seen the contract, I've got the page with all the signatures of you and your corrupt gang of councilors. I'm assuming if I give it a *really* good look through that I'll find out just how much they've paid you to rush through this process and bypass the approval of the locals."

That had his attention. I saw a muscle in his jaw clench, then relax. Clench then relax.

"What is it with people sticking their noses in?" he huffed. "Take your two cents and keep moving, Bess. I was elected, I'm in charge, that's the end of it."

"You should slap him," a tiny voice whispered from my bag.

"What did you just say?" Stephen gawped.

"Nothing. But this isn't over," I said, before I made for the door and marched back out of the building. That went well.

14

*P*epper was snoring on Kari's fire-side rug before I'd even had chance to sit down. In a state of such frustration, the only place I could think to go was my best friend's house. Given that a distracted mind had led to me removing the clothes of a septuagenarian recently, I needed to be careful incase my newfound powers took control.

Other than a short session in the garden, I'd yet to use my magic intentionally and I was genuinely nervous about what I was capable of. I wouldn't be all that surprised to find out that the town hall and the adjacent office building had burst into flames minutes after I left, or that Stephen had been found on the roof of the cathedral one town over.

"Mint tea, good for the soul, or the bowels, something like that," Kari said, mug in hand. I gratefully took the drink and let the steam from its surface add a layer of moisture to my face as I held it to my lips.

"How do you keep your anger under control?" I asked.

"I thought you were coming here with a witchy question, not an anger management problem," she laughed.

"I've brought both," I smiled, taking a sip.

"She should have killed him," Pepper muttered.

"So you *and* the kitten have rage issues, huh?" Kari smiled. "Look, everyone and their mother knows that Stephen Berry is a garbage person. He's like a leech, or some other type of slimy worm thing that just slides into any vacant seat of power and goes wild with it. He wasn't *that* bad until he won the election, you'd think he was running a country the way he lords it about over everyone."

"I don't know if it's power so much as popularity," I offered. "What power does he really have being the councilor of a small town in the Lake District? None. But everyone around here knows his name, he got enough votes to win the election that gave him the seat."

"He won because everyone hated the other guy more than they hated Steve," Kari reminded me. I already knew that, of course. My parents had been volunteering for Steve during his campaign in order to keep the other candidate out of power, now I imagined my mom was regretting the decision.

"Either way, I thought he would say something to defend himself after I confronted him about the green belt. He doesn't even care," I said.

"Well did you use your powers to blow him to pieces?"

"No!"

"Then you already did the right thing. Look, your magic can help you out in endless ways but can also, very easily, get you into trouble. Don't use your powers on humans that give you a hard time, it's a slippery slope. All we can do in this case is report it, send a letter to the prime minister or something," Kari suggested.

"You think I should write a letter to ten Downing Street and let them know that some power-mad douchebag is trying to sell off fields that house the bones of dead witches? What a fun way to get Scotland Yard knocking on my door."

"I'm trying to help, but if you'd rather talk about *other* things…" she paused.

"What have you heard?" I groaned.

"Just that you and James were seen wandering out of a hotel this morning, hand in hand, both with a rosy glow," she winked.

"What!? That's not true!"

"I'm just teasing, mostly," she laughed, sticking her tongue out at me. "All I heard was that you were coming out of the hotel and Victoria caught you both and went nuts."

"How have you heard about that?" I gasped.

"People around here are all curtain-twitchers, just aching for a little action to talk about. This has been pretty big news all day," she grinned. "I would have messaged you earlier to get the details but I wanted to hear it from the horse's mouth."

"That guy on the train tracks, we think he was murdered and the train bit was a cover up," I explained. "Sergeant Digby thinks it's a dead end, so James and I have been looking into it together. The dead guy was staying at that hotel, so we went to have a look around. That's the whole story. There was no afternoon delight, despite what you may have heard," I said, cocking an eyebrow.

"Well it would have been late-morning delight, but that's beside the point," she replied. "So the two of you are just searching for a killer together, that's the sexiest thing I've ever heard."

"What are you talking about?" I laughed. "How is that sexy?"

"You have both been pulled back together by the universe, it's incredibly hot. If you can't see it then I don't know what to tell you," she said. She leaned back in her chair and stared at the ceiling for a moment. "Callum was asking after you again."

"Was he now?" I groaned. Callum was Kari's friend, or maybe that was overstating their relationship. Kari worked as a personal trainer in the local gym, something that she'd done on and off for years. Her real passion in life was yet to be determined, but this was a good stop-gap and the pay was good.

When I was in London she would message me to ask if I'd moved my body that week other than the journey to and from the train station. She poked and prodded until I agreed to go out for a walk or follow a yoga video online. Since I'd been back she'd tried to convince me to go hiking several times and I'd always been busy with work, but I knew she'd start pushing again soon, especially now I was in on the secret of Black Bridge.

Callum worked out at her gym. He was good looking, if you were into the chiseled male physique that is. We'd vaguely known each other from around town, he was a handy man and seemed to turn his skills to any task with ease. I'd interacted with him only a few times, but he had really taken a shine to me if Kari's stories were anything to go by.

"I am super single and I don't mind being the one to say it, I'm pretty hot," Kari sighed. "You have this weird thing going on with James, but I am free as a bird. But who does Callum want to spend time with? You!"

"How does my name come up? I don't understand it. Is he a stalker?" I teased.

"Don't speak of my handsome Callum like that," she laughed. "No, I just asked him if he was seeing anyone and he shrugged, said he'd love to get hold of *your* number though. The world is a cruel and unusual place."

"Well I am technically single," I countered. "I mean, not even just technically, I'm *totally* single. Would it be crazy to give him my number?"

"To make James jealous you mean? Like, to push him into breaking up with Vic and coming running to your door in the middle of the night with a bouquet of roses and a bottle of wine?"

"He ran off with Victoria, he's with her," I said.

"But he wants to be with you!"

"We're old news, I don't think it's a good idea to be even entertaining it as a possibility. I broke his heart, broke my own heart too if I'm being honest," I sulked. "I know you're holding out hope to be witness to this big romantic reunion, but it's not happening. Victoria shouted something about a train ticket and he chased her down the street."

"Ah, the ticket," Kari nodded.

"Okay, now you have my attention," Pepper mewed, legs stretched long in front of his tiny, fuzzy body. "You know something about this ticket and it looks like it might get interesting."

"What?" I laughed, then looked at Kari who had a concerned expression. "Wait, is he right?"

"If I tell you about it, you can't have a total melt down. Promise?" she said, now sitting forward and wringing her hands anxiously.

"Tell me!" I insisted. I was making no such promise.

"After you left, maybe a week later, James came to see me. I was packing to head back to Maryland and he came to the house in a panic, he looked pale and wide-eyed. I knew something was going on with him, so I let him in and he wouldn't sit down, just pacing the floor."

I felt as though every sound that had been humming away in the background fell silent. All I wanted to know was what happened next.

"He asked me where exactly you were, the address of your new apartment," Kari continued.

"Why?"

"Well you'd obviously fought about him coming with you, he'd decided to stay and then you'd disappeared. He'd not wanted to talk about the upcoming move, he was trying to delay the inevitable but ignoring it. He knew where you would be working and the part of London you were moving to, but not the full address."

"Why did he need my address?"

"He changed his mind, Liz," Kari said. I felt my heart sink. "He didn't want to be here without you and he wanted to follow you there, I told him everything he needed to know, helped him find the closest train station to your new place and—"

She cut herself off. Pepper jumped onto the arm of the chair and headbutted her shoulder.

"I helped him buy a train ticket. They don't have the digital machines at the Black Bridge station so he had to wait for the physical tickets to arrive in the mail."

"He was coming to London," I said, my hearing seeming to dip in and out as if I couldn't stand to hear another word of it. "But he didn't come, I don't understand."

"His dad had a fall, a bad one. I think he tripped over outside and hit his head on something, he was in the hospital for weeks. He

131

needed more help around the house and I guess it was too much for his mom to do alone, so James stayed for them."

Was now an appropriate time to scream? Should I cry? Maybe I could try to use my newfound witch powers to make an enormous pile of chocolate eclairs appear and just gorge myself until I black out. James was going to come to London. He changed his mind. I couldn't believe it. I'd been in my cheap, crappy apartment crying myself to sleep over our breakup but it hadn't really been over yet.

But Victoria said she found the train ticket, so that must mean he kept it? I might throw up.

"Do you have anything to drink?" I asked.

"Do you want hard liquor?" she countered.

"Just *something.*"

She leapt up out of her chair and rushed into the kitchen before reappearing with a large bottle of brandy. I was fairly certain that Kari wasn't a brandy drinker, I don't think I'd ever drank a drop of the stuff, but I would take what I could get. I needed to take the edge off this revelation before I spiraled downwards.

"Oh!" she tutted, snapping her fingers. Two brandy glasses appeared on the coffee table in front of her and she dutifully poured us both a double. The smell was not something I was used to, and the taste made my eyes water, but I think the love of my life had slipped through my fingers, tried to get back to me, then slipped through them again. I *needed* a drink.

Kari did what any good friend would do on an afternoon when someone's heart is broken. She shut the curtains, turned on the TV and loaded up her copy of Legally Blonde so that we could recite every scene from memory in time with Reese Witherspoon.

"How is this movie only ninety-six minutes. I bet they cut a bunch of stuff out and honestly if this was one of those, like *crazy* long movies people would still watch it," Kari complained. "Titanic is one hundred and ninety-five minutes long, that is over three hours! How many times have we watched that?"

"Easily a million," I replied.

"Exactly! *Jack? Jack? I won't let go, I promise',*" she performed. "That's probably days of my life I've spent watched Rose getting steamy with Jack in that car, and they couldn't add a few hours onto Legally Blonde?"

"They did sequels," I offer.

"Pssh," she dismissed. I look at the time and realize I'm supposed to be home to eat with James. Was that still happening? Who knows, I don't think I could even face him at this point. What would I say? Am I allowed to know about the train ticket? Will Kari tell him she told me? This is a mess.

"I need to get going," I said, beckoning Pepper back away from the rug and gesturing for him to jump back into the satchel. He'd been interested in watching the movie but the title sequence had barely finished and he was snoring.

"Should I give Callum your number? Because if you truly want nothing to do with him then maybe I should make a move," Kari smiled.

"I thought you *had* been trying to make moves."

"Ouch, I'll need some cream for that burn. Jeez," she grimaced. "Why not exchange numbers, text a little, see if you like talking with him and if there is nothing there then at least you know."

"I thought you were hoping for a big James and Lizzie romance to strike up again."

"Yeah, ideally I would be picking out my dress for your wedding already, but you guys have so much history that I don't know if either of you could let it go. I know that sounds harsh but—"

"No, you're right. Okay, give Callum my number, but if he starts sending me photos of his, you know, stuff... then I'm blocking him," I grin.

"No pictures of Callum junior, got it!"

"Urgh, don't call it that," I groan, opening the front door. "See you later!"

"Bye, Liz, let me know if I need to buy a dress for your wedding to Callum so I can get looking online!"

"Why is she in charge of your love life?" Pepper asked, sticking his head out from the top of the satchel.

"Because she's bored, mostly," I replied. "Maybe if I set *her* up on a date then she will stay out of my business."

"You can't use love magic, just FYI. I know TV makes it look like a thing that you can just do whenever you like, but that isn't how real life works. If you start messing with people's free will then you're basically playing God and I don't think you're anywhere near advanced enough to deal with the fallout of using magic like that."

"Good to know, thanks." I rolled my eyes. Maybe a bath would wash off the day and I could practice some small spells with Pepper, he could teach me the make-over magic he's used on me a couple of times and I could try and breathe life into the dying houseplants that are littering my bedroom.

The streets were dark and quiet. Most people were anchored to their sofas watching their nightly dose of TV shows and the flashing lights were visible through the curtains of every window. A car or two rolled by, the clouds had kept little of the day's heat trapped down here so the air was biting, nipping at my face.

Pepper was snug inside the satchel, wrapped in his thick fur coat, oblivious to the chill. When I got close enough to the house to see it I stopped in my tracks. The door was open. My grandmother was out with her friends, my grandfather was still roaming the Greek seas by himself, and I was the only other person with a key.

"Hey, wake up," I said, jostling the satchel enough to rouse the sleeping cat.

"What?!" he replied groggily.

"Someone's broken into the house."

"Huh?" he stuck his head out of the bag and looked down the street. "How can you tell that from here?"

I took another few steps toward the house. I knew someone had been in there, I just knew it. What if there was still someone inside? A dangerous stranger lying in wait for me to return and then… "I'm calling the police," I announced.

I wasn't calling just *any* old police officer, I was planning to call just one. I pulled out my phone and scrolled through my contacts, hoping that, if I was really lucky, James hadn't changed his number in all the years since I'd last spoken with him. It rang a few times, then the call was picked up.

"Hello?" a voice answered. I let out a sigh of relief. It was him.

"Hey, it's Liz. Look, I know it's dumb and I shouldn't be calling you, but—"

"Are you okay?" he interrupted. I could hear the worry in his voice.

"Yeah, but I think someone's broken into the house, they might still be there."

"Don't go inside, I'm on the way." He hung up and I found myself staring at the front door, almost urging who ever had busted the lock to come walking out so I could put a face on the mystery assailant.

"Can't you use magic to protect the house or something?" I ask.

"No, but *you* could. Not yet obviously, you're like a baby with a handgun at this point, but eventually you'll be able to wield that weapon with confidence," Pepper replied.

"Baby with a handgun? You couldn't think of a better analogy?"

"Hey, someone could be stealing all of the food from the cupboards in there, I'm very stressed right now," he exclaimed.

"People don't really break in to steal food," I grumbled.

I heard running feet and turned to see James racing down the street toward me. "Are you okay? Are you hurt?" he wheezed. All those daily jogs had paid off as he had made it across town in record time.

"I'm fine, I've barely moved an inch since I called you."

"Stay here," he said, stretching a protective arm across the space in front of me to keep me back. He walked to the doorway, peered inside, then listened carefully for any sign of movement. He disappeared into the house and returned minutes later with a strange look on his face.

"What?"

"There's no one in there," he replied. "The door looks busted, but nothing's missing as far as I can see. Your TV is still there, that's usually the first thing to go..."

"They didn't take anything?"

"They might have gotten spooked and ran away, maybe someone caught them in the act," he offered. I don't know if that was supposed

135

to sound comforting, that I hadn't been robbed, but I felt all the more tense about it now. What if they came back to finish the job? "You should sit down before you fall down," he said, rushing to my side to place an arm around my waist as my knees buckled beneath me.

"It's not safe, I can't lock the door now," I muttered.

"I'll fix it," he said. We stepped inside and I looked at my home, the place I'd spent every night for months and had memorized. Everything was exactly the same. Why break the door down but not take anything? James half-carried me to the sofa and lowered me down, Pepper bounced out of the satchel to avoid being sat on and I could see his shiny cat eyes surveying the room.

"What if they come back?" I asked, my voice almost shaking.

"That won't happen, because I'm going to be here," he said, crouching down so we were at eye-level. "I'll order us some food, because I sprinted over here without the fajita stuff I promised I was bringing, and we'll eat. No one from the station will be over here before morning anyway, you're getting the VIP treatment."

"Thank you," I replied sincerely. James stood up and walked to the door to assess the damage and Pepper blew out what looked like a small smoke ring, which swirled into a heart shape before dissipating. James was spending the night? What would the neighbors say?

15

---

*W*hen I woke up it seemed my brain graced me with almost five entire seconds before the events of the previous night came crashing back into the forefront of my thoughts.

James had spent the night on the couch. I knew that version of events would be dismissed by Kari, Deanna and just about every other person in town, but it was the truth. We'd ordered curry, naan breads and rice from an Indian restaurant one town over. It used to be one of my favorite places to eat and James had remembered.

They charged five pounds for delivery due to our location in Black Bridge, but when the food is so good it's hard to care. Even now the house was thick with the scent of the spices in the sauce. Pepper was still completely asleep, so I gently climbed out of bed and pulled open the curtains to stare out at the start of another day.

The streets were more alive now than they had been on the walk back from Kari's place last night. The thought of being here in the daylight didn't seem as scary now, but today would involve getting the locks fixed and maybe investing in a security camera, finances permitting.

James had managed to reattach the chain across the door where it had been retched from the screws, and placed something heavy up against the wood so that no one would be able to get inside even if they wanted to. His presence in the house had been enough to make me feel safe, although I knew that our little sleepover wouldn't have gone unnoticed.

I must have left my phone downstairs, because I was certain that someone must have noticed James coming over last night and spread the word. If news had gotten out then Kari would have sent no less than five hundred text messages by now.

What day was it? Was I supposed to be in the restaurant? That would be another reason to track down my phone because if I was on the rota and hadn't shown up, my mom would only ring twice before showing up at the door. I didn't want her seeing James in here, I'd never hear the end of it.

I hadn't had the freedom to practice magic last night because James had been there, so there was no way I was going to be able to improve my appearance without doing it manually. Pepper had made his position quite clear on the matter and I wasn't going to push it. I ran a comb through my hair, changed into a pair of dusty green, cotton trousers and a pale grey t-shirt and headed for the stairs.

I couldn't hear movement in the living room, and I briefly considered that James might still be asleep. A pounding on the front door put a swift end to that idea. From the top step I was able to see James drag the giant wooden chest of drawers away from the front door, slide the chain across and let in an officer that I didn't recognize.

At this point I began to descend and the two of them looked at me. "Ms. Sutton, this is Officer Dunne, and Officer Mitchell is just outside. They will be handling the incident for you," James said, barely making eye contact with me.

"Hi," I offered, slightly confused. James already had his shoes on, he stepped out of the house to the street and that was it. What had happened? He'd slept on the sofa, we'd been laughing and talking for hours last night, eating our takeout with the radio on and— had I said something I shouldn't?

I'd only had that one glass of brandy at Kari's house, and that had been *before* we watched Legally Blonde. By the time I'd realized my house had been busted into I felt sober, completely in control of my faculties. I know I didn't mention the train ticket, even though it had been on my mind. I didn't mention Victoria, or London. Maybe the whole thing had been a little flirty, sure, but why would he be taking off without a word?

My phone buzzed on the coffee table and I walked down the remaining steps to see what it wanted. The two police officers stepped into the living room. Officer Mitchell had a camera in his hand, presumably he'd taken photographs from outside before they entered.

My phone had a missed call and a text message, that was all. I had anticipated a flurry of messages from Kari begging for juicy details, but evidently, she hadn't caught wind of my house guest yet. The missed call was from my mother, she had tried to call but I'd taken too long to get down the stairs and she'd hung up, not bothering to leave a voicemail. No doubt she'd rock up outside any minute and ask a million questions about the police presence, the break in... you name it.

The text message went some way to explaining James' unusual exit, however. It was from Callum, the entire message was visible on my lock screen beneath the missed call notification.

'Hey Liz, it's Callum. I've been trying to think of the best opening line I could think of, and I've settled on this one (I'm trying to get into your good books!). I went to school with David Dawson and have a million embarrassing stories about him, would you be interested in hearing a few over coffee? X'

So my ex-boyfriend decided to spend the night in my house to protect me, after I'd learned the lengths he went to years ago to try and restore our relationship, and he wakes up to a text-message buzzing into my inbox from a guy that I have clearly just given my number to. Okay, now the walking off in a huff makes a little more sense.

"Ms. Sutton, we have some questions for you when you're ready," Officer Dunne said, giving me a sympathetic smile that I'm sure was to reassure me that everything was okay. The problems I had right now weren't going to be something that these two guys could help me with.

Before I'd even opened my mouth to respond, my mother was bursting through the open front door and shrieking loudly at all three of us. "Elizabeth! Why are the police here? Did you kill someone? What happened? When you didn't answer the phone I knew that something bad must have happened, is she going to prison?!" she screamed. Well *this* outburst was unlikely to make this morning run smoothly.

"If you don't tell me every sordid little detail I am going to freak out," Deanna cried, wrapping up a tuna melt sandwich to go for the old guy that runs the pharmacy down the street. My mom had shown up at the house to drag me to my shift, I'd lost track of the days this week and getting back into journalist-mode had meant that I'd mentally put the restaurant job to one side.

It had been ten thirty when I finally got there, Deanna and my dad had been left alone to serve customers as my mom ran off to track me down, then insisted on staying for the entire conversation with the police. I told them that nothing appeared to be missing, that was all I could say with certainty. Nothing looked different downstairs, but upstairs…

I didn't tell the officers, because I didn't really have the words to describe my hunch, but something about my bedroom this morning had looked off. When I woke up and got out of bed, I just *sensed* it, but couldn't actually identify anything specific. On the hurried march back to the restaurant my mom had ranted about intuition and that I should always trust my gut. That hadn't helped much.

"Liz!" Natasha yelled as she walked through the door. If she was also here to talk to me about James then I might just put my head in the oven.

"Hey, you here for some lunch?" I asked.

"Sure, could I get a ham salad sandwich and a coffee bigger than my head?" she laughed, rummaging through her purse for money. I set about slicing the bread, pointing to various salad items and having her nod approval at the ones she wanted while Deanna made the drink.

"Rough day at work?" I asked.

"Urgh, you have no idea. I'm getting whiplash from Stephen coming in and changing everything he wants from the project," she huffed.

"What do you mean?"

"Well he said that the retail park website can be put on the back burner for now, but to set up a site for his re-election campaign, he wanted newsletter sign ups, big bright colors, a place where constituents could donate to the cause," she rolled her eyes. Since when did Stephen care about being re-elected?

"When did he tell you all this?" I asked.

"This morning! He just marched in and started listing demands, that I shouldn't respond to any queries from Diversity Capital about the retail site for now because they are dealing with a lot, I told him it was none of my business, so long as I get paid!" she grinned.

I had a moment of realization and my jaw fell open. My mom was, once again, sitting out of sight with a magazine in her hands and her feet up. "I need to leave," I announced, having handed over Natasha's lunch and begun removing my apron.

"Because?" she said, not glancing away from the gossip rag she was reading.

"I think I know how to stop the green belt sale," I said. That wasn't *technically* the truth, but it wasn't a total lie either. Somewhere in the middle.

"What?! Then go, why are you still here?!" she shrieked. I grabbed my bag from the hooks and burst through the back door of the restaurant and began marching to the offices beside the town hall. I knew now why my bedroom looked different, something *had* been taken from my house. It was the signed copy of the contract that could tie Councilor Stephen Berry to the sale. It was dated, which meant that it was proof he'd agreed to sell the land before speaking to the residents about it.

Maybe I wouldn't have figured it out eventually, but Natasha helped it all fall into place. Stephen did want to get re-elected, he'd had a taste of power and didn't want to relinquish it now. He'd been awful at his job since he won the last election, there was no way his performance record was going to help his efforts to keep his seat, but this deal with Diversity Capital could be the end of his career.

I'd told him I had it, now the contract was MIA. I burst into the reception area and got a weary glance from Election Ellen, peering over the monitor of her computer and knitting her brows together as she regarded my entrance.

"You again," she said, not a question or a statement really, just a disgruntled comment from a disgruntled government employee.

"Is Stephen here?" I asked.

"Councilor Berry?" she said, correcting me without making a scene of it.

"Yeah, is he in?" I didn't want to wait for an answer because it looked as though she were about to get to her feet and shuffle towards me. I knew the way already, I didn't need her to guide me there.

"Hey you can't just—" I had already stormed down the hallway and door shutting in my wake cut Ellen off mid-sentence.

The look on Stephen's face when I threw open his office door was one I wish I'd photographed. There was a small yellow sharps bin on his desk and the grinding sound of a shredder just out of view. I would bet good money that the tiny strips of paper falling into the waste basket were from the damming contract baring his signature.

"You shouldn't be in here," he remarked, without a hint of irony.

"You shouldn't have broken into my house, I guess we're even."

"Why ruin my life over something so trivial?" he said. I figured he might at least try to deny it, but maybe he was past lying at this point. "I could call off the deal now, announce myself as the savior of the green belt and be lorded as a hero in this town. No one has to know."

"Are you kidding? You broke into my home and took something, that's a crime. Not to mention whatever payout you got for going behind everyone's back with Diversity Capital. Urgh, you're such a snake," I grimaced.

"I've shredded it now, and I didn't leave a single fingerprint anywhere in the house because I was wearing surgical gloves, so good luck proving anything," he smirked. He was so smug, I wanted to wipe that grin off his punch-able little face.

"You don't think that Lionel would have made copies for the head office back in the states?" I said. That took the edge off his triumph, I could see it. I couldn't help but laugh at him, his desperation to keep a tight grip on a councilor seat in the middle of the Lake District could lead him to breaking into my house for a stupid contract?

"Well he's dead now, so I don't really think it matters," he muttered.

Why would Stephen just own a pair of surgical gloves? He had just bragged about it as the reason why he didn't leave any fingerprints in my house, but maybe he had another pair that he worn after the town hall meeting.

The shredding of the papers had left a fine dust on his desk. I watched as he reached into a drawer, pulled out a mini vacuum cleaner and sucked up the mess, then spritzing disinfectant on the wood before buffing it with a paper towel. I looked again at the yellow sharps bin, thought about him telling me he was counting his carbs the other day. I couldn't understand what I was seeing, but I had a suspicion that it was all pointing to one thing.

"You killed him," I muttered, as if testing out the sound of it to my own ear before letting it be heard by someone else.

"What?" he said, still rubbing the paper towel in tight circles against the desk's surface.

"You killed Lionel after you saw how the town hall went, you knew that you hadn't convinced anyone that it was a good idea so you tried to back out to protect your reputation," I gasped.

"You don't know what you're talking about, he parked on the tracks, idiot got hit by a car. Maybe they don't have crossings like that down in London and he got confused."

"He was dead before the train hit."

Stephen let out a long sigh and put the disinfectant spray back into a drawer. I heard an unusual rubbery sound, like a balloon stretching, and realized that he was putting on more surgical gloves.

"The police didn't care enough to look into it, so why are you?" he said, now on his feet and walking around the desk toward me. "It was just a few stupid fields, it would have made me rich. Now I have to cut you out of the picture, too."

Too? He had to mean Lionel. I was standing in a room with a killer, how had I gotten myself into this mess. I reached a hand behind me, not for the door handle, but for the phone in my back pocket. I unlocked it with my thumb print and prayed that I could navigate the home screen from memory. I went to my call list, knowing that the top of that list would be my mom's name from when she rang about my lateness.

I moved my thumb down half an inch and tapped.

"Cut me out of the picture?" I repeated.

"When you're ambitious like me, Bess," my skin shuddered at the sound of the nickname, "you are willing to do what it takes to get to the top. That's why you never succeeded in London, your failure is a reflection of your lack of determination. I am going to get to the top, and I won't let you, or Lionel Basset, or some stupid acres of grass mess that up for me."

A sound behind me let me know that help was thundering along the corridor, so I simply stepped to the right suddenly. Stephen took it as a sign of an escape attempt, so lunged at me at the precise moment that the office door swung open. The edge of the door smashed into his nose and he screamed an almost animalistic sound, blood now streaming down his upper lip.

James grabbed me. Officer Dunne and Officer Mitchell were standing in the doorway, slightly stunned.

"Him, 'cuff him," James ordered. The officers did as they were told.

"How did you get here so quickly?" I asked.

"Ellen called to say a woman had just stormed down to the councilor's office and that she felt threatened and feared for the safety of everyone in the building," he explained.

"What?"

"Yeah, dramatic I know, but when she described who it was I knew it was you. I ran over here and then when you called I—I heard everything he said Liz, that confession was as good as anything. He's done for, I'm just glad you're—" he cut himself off. I sank into the embrace as Stephen Berry was dragged down the corridor, his shrieks of pain growing distant.

I had been in real danger. I could have been killed in here. Shouldn't my magic have intervened? James helped me to my feet.

"Should I call someone for you?" he asked.

"I'll call Kari, it's okay," I said. He turned to leave the office first as I brought my phone up to my face ready to search for her number.

That was odd. That call I'd made to James, the one I tried to orchestrate behind my back, wasn't recorded on the screen. The call didn't happen. I'd accidentally called my own house number and was currently on voicemail to myself.

But somehow, despite calling the wrong number my phone had connected to James and saved my life.

Maybe my magic had intervened after all.

16

*J*t turns out no one likes bad press. When David Dawson finally returned from his Prague trip, I demanded that he take me on full time, presenting a huge article about the Lionel Basset murder as my bargaining chip. I now report full time for The Herald and, hopefully, will never have to work a shift in my parent's restaurant again.

When the article was published, someone must have sent a copy to the Diversity Capital headquarters – it was me – and they quickly backed out of the acquisition proposal as their stock prices had taken a hit. They had tried to go into business with a killer, it's a bad look for a company apparently.

I had half expected that my efforts to save the green belt, successful efforts may I add, would have garnered the adoration of my mother for at least an entire afternoon, but no. I was offered a half-hearted 'Good for you, Elizabeth', and we would be unlikely to mention it again.

My grandmother was a little more generous with her praise. My grandparents had followed through with their plans to stop the endless cruises for a while and move back to Black Bridge, apparently training me up to use my magic was a full-family endeavor.

"Are you sure you want to do this?" Pepper asked, his mouth twisted into a grimace as he sat on the vanity table looking at me.

"It's my turn to try," I nodded.

"If you burn your eyebrows off then I want it on the record that I thought this was a bad idea," he groaned. "Do you remember what I said to do?"

"Yes, just focus." I looked into the mirror and tried to channel all my energy into what my face would look like with simple – but still smoking hot – make up. I had a date this afternoon and I was filled with excitement and nerves.

After several moments of trying, it looked as though I had a thin slick of eyeliner and darker lashes. My complexion was a little more even with a subtle blush on the apple of each cheek. It wasn't much, but I'd done it all on my own. I was thrilled. Pepper made an impressed noise then jumped over to the bed.

"What are you wearing? I didn't think I was going to care, but now I'm dying to know," Pepper mewed.

"I'm wearing this," I said. I stood up and turned around so he could get the full picture. It was a dark grey t-shirt with the names of the main characters from Buffy written in large letters, *'Buffy & Angel & Spike & Giles & Willow & Xander...'*

My shirt was cute, folded a little on the sleeves and tucked into my best pair of jeans. I hadn't picked shoes yet, but I thought I looked good. Pepper stared at me, wordlessly, for almost ten seconds before responding.

"This show that you like so much, when was it on TV?" he asked.

"Well it *first* aired in the late nineties, but if you have the right channels you can watch it whenever you like," I replied.

"...Right," he nodded. I wasn't necessarily looking for his approval, but not getting it felt like a blow. There was a knock at the door and I bounced down the stairs to see who it was. Standing outside was Officer James Webster.

"Hi," I smiled.

"Could I come in?" he asked. I nodded and he walked into the living room and sat down. "I just thought you'd want an update about the case."

"Yeah, is this on the record?" I said, glancing around the room for my phone so I could record the conversation.

"Not exactly, we'll put out a press release this week. There's just been a lot to deal with," he sighed, running a hand through his hair. "Stephen confessed to killing Lionel, the confession took a while because he was sobbing so hard we could barely understand a word he was saying."

"I bet that was fun to watch," I smirked.

"Well the guy has always been awful, so there was an element of schadenfreude to it," he smiled. "He said that the town hall meeting made it pretty clear that there was no way he was going to win everybody over, he spoke to Lionel about calling off the whole deal and Lionel laughed in his face."

"I bet he hated that."

"Oh yeah, he said that Lionel then tried to jump into his Bentley and drive away, talking about contracts and lawyers and blah blah blah. Stephen said he asked if they could talk it out, managed to get an invite into the car and that's when it all happened, he killed him and then panicked, thought the train would cover up what he'd done."

"What *did* he do?"

"Well Stephen is diabetic, type one. He's also a little germophobic it seems, so he pulled on a pair of gloves that he carries with him all the time, choked Lionel until he passed out and then injected him with insulin, a *lot* of it. I think the train slowing down so quickly messed up his plans," he explained. "Digby is in a world of trouble, they are talking about stripping him of his title, demoting him."

"Who would be in charge around here?"

"They were thinking that I might be a good candidate, I haven't given them an answer on it yet," he said. I could see that he wanted me to give an opinion. I shuffled along the sofa so that I could reach a hand out to him as he leaned forward in the armchair.

"You should do it, you'd be great. Sergeant Webster has a good ring to it after all," I laughed.

"Vic said that if her career takes off and we have to move that it would be harder for me to leave town if I was Sergeant."

Victoria and James were still together, despite her being absolutely awful and most of the town thinking they should split. I had been in that camp for a while, but I had a date with Callum in an hour and I was trying to stay out of James' business. I had broken his heart, the decent thing to do would be to let him see how he really feels about me being home. I owe him time.

"Just because you're dating, doesn't mean you have to take job advice from her," I warned. "I think you should go for it, you'd make a great sergeant and I think you could make a real difference around here. Say yes, worry about the details later."

He held my hand. For a moment we could have been eighteen again, and maybe no matter who we were seeing or where our lives were at we would always feel like this. He flinched suddenly, as if I'd given him a static shock. Had I just zapped him with my magic? That would be something to speak to Pepper about later.

"I'm glad you're home, Liz," he said. "Black Bridge suits you."

"I'm glad to *be* home." I had initially considered this a retreat, a soldier that had managed to advance the front line all the way to the capital city but then had to fall back, scurry to the starting point.

Maybe this wasn't a failure. I was working full time as a journalist now, admittedly it was for the Black Bridge Herald, but it was still paid work in the field I was passionate about. James could be sergeant, too. Life had finally taken us where we wanted to go, but just not together like we'd always imagined. That stung.

"You look like you're going somewhere special," he said, restoring his police hat to the top of his head as he stood to leave.

"I have a date," I admitted, worried that his reaction might not be a positive one.

"Callum?" he asked. I nodded. "Yeah, Kari might have let it slip a few days ago."

"Great," I said as I rolled my eyes. "I wish I'd been able to tell you myself."

"It's fine, you deserve to be with someone that makes you happy."

"So do you," I said, pointedly. His expression changed, his jaw clenched. I had no idea where this would all go, maybe we were going to get back together at some point, maybe not. I think there was still a fight to be had, some explosive argument where I confront him about the train ticket and why he didn't call me when his dad got ill. I would have come back, he must have known that, or had he just hated me too much at that point?

"Bye, Liz." And just like that, he was gone. The door closed behind him and I was left in the living room alone thinking of all the things I should have said.

"You really brought the goods," I laughed, tears swelling in both eyes.

"I told you, I have a million of these," Callum nodded. He really did know more embarrassing stories about David Dawson than I knew what to do with. I'd just been informed that David had wet himself, on stage, in the middle of a nativity play at school when he was playing the role of one of the wise men. He had stepped forward, opened his mouth in preparation to deliver his line, and a dark patch had appeared on his costume.

"What did he say?" I asked.

"Well *his* character had brought the baby the gift of gold," Callum explained. "So as the stain on his white robes grew he announced that he'd put the gold in his pocket and it must have melted. I thought the teacher was going to have a heart attack she was laughing so hard."

I tried to compose myself enough to take another sip of my coffee, but I was struggling. I hadn't laughed so hard in a long time and Callum had been so skilled at keeping the conversation going that I hadn't even realized how long we'd been sat here. My drink was cold, probably had been for twenty minutes at that point, but I didn't care.

I hadn't been in this coffee shop since I'd moved back to town, I had been trying to avoid being seen in public by my ex-boyfriend in case it prompted an uncomfortable conversation. This place was exactly the same as I remembered it, the sound of coffee beans being ground by the machine in the back, the smell of the roast, the photographs of the building in all its forms over the last one hundred and fifty years.

The door opened as my cousins, Deanna and Marla, walked in and looked around for an empty table. Marla's baby was due soon, I couldn't remember the exact date but I knew that before long there would be a new lease of life in the family. It felt like all of us were moving forward along our own path.

Deanna spotted me, glanced at the handsome man I was sat with, then smiled. I knew she was rooting for James and I to rekindle things, but more than anything she was rooting for me, just me.

"Would you like another drink?" Callum asked.

"Yeah, that would be great," I replied.

"Same?"

"Sure!" I nodded. He stood up and walked back over to the counter to get us a fresh round of beverages to extend our date. I had been nervous about whether we'd have anything in common, about what we'd say to each other, but I found myself amazed at how natural it had all felt. James and I had a history, good or bad, but this... this was new. A clean slate.

My phone pinged, a notification to alert me to an email from David. I had an assignment, some fluff piece about the local hiking trails that he wanted me to get started with asap. He also said to keep on the Lionel Basset investigation, that he wanted me to keep the readership of The Herald updated with every step of Stephen's trial when it came to it.

I gazed out of the window at the street, Ernie walking back to his shop with a sandwich in hand that he'd no doubt bought from my dad just moments earlier. Somewhere in the distance a train rumbled away from the station, and I remembered how only days ago I'd considered trying to chase it down so I could climb aboard and start fresh somewhere else.

This place had felt like the dead end I'd needed to escape from. Now it felt like the most hopeful place I could be.

THANKS FOR READING

Thanks for reading, I hope you enjoyed the book.

It would really help me out if you could leave an honest review with your thoughts and rating on Amazon. Every bit of feedback helps!

Book 2 coming soon! x

MAILING LIST

Want to be notified when I release my latest book? Join my mailing list. It's for new releases only. No spam.

http://eepurl.com/gIHYJj